If Goliath Dickman hadn't had the most loving and supportive parents he could ever imagine—and he's seen plenty of depravity during his years on the force—he would have thought his parents hated him. After all, how could they have named him what they did? Goliath would never tarnish the memory of his beloved mother by saying such a thing out loud, however. So when the opportunity arises, he transfers to a deputy position in a small town.

After losing his temper on the first day—thank goodness they'd been understanding guys—Goliath asks the others to call him Ollie, and he settles in at his new place in his new town. He runs across Earl Raukus at a local restaurant and finds himself enamored with the pretty, brown-eyed blond. Unfortunately, Goliath spots Earl laughing and chatting with a black-haired guy across the room, and his hopes are dashed.

Imagine Goliath's confusion when Earl continues flirting with him. Uncertain, he switches to his default—he clams up, responding curtly. Confused by the hurt that fills Earl's eyes, Goliath tracks him down . . . and discovers something the town can't possibly want getting out. Could the world of shifters truly be real, and what would be his place within it?

What is Not in a Name
Copyright © 2022 Charlie Richards
ISBN: 978-1-4874-3756-5
Cover art by Angela Waters

Published by eXtasy Books Inc

Look for us online at:
www.eXtasybooks.com

# What is Not in a Name
# Wolves of Stone Ridge 60

## By

## Charlie Richards

# DEDICATION

*Don't ask what else could go wrong? You won't like the answer.*
*~Me*

# CHAPTER ONE

"How was your first week, Ollie?"

Pausing in his stroll across the relatively quiet bullpen, Goliath Dickman turned toward Sheriff Anthony Holsteen. He saw the way the slender male leaned one shoulder against the doorframe to his office. The sheriff's hands were shoved into the pockets of his jeans, and he sported a small relaxed smile.

"Uh, good . . . mostly," Goliath replied, and he did his best not to cringe at how tentative his deep voice sounded.

"Mostly?" Anthony quirked one brow up questioningly. The man looked beyond Goliath for a second, obviously surveying who was in the room. Returning his attention to Goliath, he narrowed his eyes and asked, "Someone bothering you?"

Goliath knew that only Deputy Markus Reussmin was in the room. The other deputy was manning the phones. Evidently, in order to speak so freely, Anthony didn't think Markus would be the person who was bothering him.

In fact, no one was bothering him.

Quickly shaking his head, Goliath dispelled that notion. "Oh, no, Sheriff," he replied. With a wince, he admitted, "Just still feel bad about the, uh" — he could feel his cheeks heat, but he continued gamely —"the Nathan incident."

On Goliath's first day, fellow deputy Nathan Kaldwell had teased him about his name, asking him if he lived up to it. He did, not that he intended to tell his co-workers that. The teasing about his name had been one of the reasons Goliath had moved from a precinct in Nashville. To face the very same problem on his first day had spiked Goliath's nearly non-existent temper.

Goliath had grabbed Nathan by the neck with one hand and used the forearm of his other to pin the man to the wall. He'd snarled in the man's face, ordering him to shut the fuck up. Deputy Nereo and Sheriff Anthony had needed to drag him away from Nathan, who'd apologized through his coughing as he'd caught his breath.

Goliath had immediately felt like shit and had begun to apologize, too. At Anthony's questioning, he'd explained what had triggered his response. Then Goliath had requested that they all call him Ollie.

Stepping away from the doorway, Anthony patted him on the upper arm. "Try to move past it, Ollie," the sheriff encouraged. "We have."

"Thanks, Sheriff," Goliath replied, nodding. "I'm tryin.'"

"I know Nathan doesn't hold it against you," Markus piped up from behind him, and Goliath pivoted to include the other deputy in the conversation. The strawberry-blond grinned at him from where he sat across the room. "But if you're so concerned about it, offer to buy Nathan a beer at the pub."

"Pub?" Goliath parroted. With a shrug, he admitted, "I'm still not too familiar with locations around here. Working on it."

In fact, Goliath appreciated the hours out on patrol, since it helped him learn street names and business locations.

"*Spiron's Bar and Grill* is the local watering hole," Markus told him, relaxing back in his chair. He crossed his ankles before him as he added, "And *Caribou's* is the local steakhouse. Both open at eleven and serve lunch and dinner."

"*Mama's Diner* is open for breakfast and lunch," Anthony added, having returned to leaning against the door frame.

"Their coffee is decent, but don't try their lattés," he warned, making a face. "If you want a latté, go to *Miss Martha's Muffins*. It's a bakery across from the elementary school."

"Just don't get their black coffee." It was Markus's turn to cringe. "Her bear claws are excellent, however."

Goliath couldn't help the soft chuckle that escaped him, and the tension that had knotted up his shoulders began to ease. "Coffee at *Mama's Diner*. Lattés and bear claws at *Martha's*." With a crooked forefinger, Goliath tipped his cowboy hat farther up his head. "And *Spiron's* is a great bar with pub food, and *Caribou's* is for date night."

Markus barked a laugh. "You got it."

Appreciating their open acceptance and levity, Goliath smiled as he glanced between his new boss and co-worker. He knew he was going to enjoy this place's laid-back attitude. When he'd applied to the small town force, he'd thought that any place would be better than his old precinct's toxic atmosphere.

*This will be so much more than better.*

"I think I'll take you up on that idea and ask Nathan about a beer," Goliath admitted as he started toward the front door. "Even if Nathan isn't holding a grudge, it'll make me feel better, at least."

Anthony dipped his chin in a nod. "And who passes up a free beer, right?"

Goliath chuckled as he shrugged. "Guess there's always a right circumstance for that." He could even think of a few, considering the frenemies he'd had in his old precinct. Not wanting to explain, Goliath ignored both men's questioning looks. "See you around."

"Have a good weekend," Anthony encouraged.

At the same time, Markus waved.

As soon as the door closed, as if on cue, Goliath's phone rang. He pulled his cell from his inside pocket. Checking the screen, he saw that it was his father—Barton.

3

Goliath smiled as he connected. "Hey, Dad."

"Hi, Goliath," his father greeted warmly. "How was your first week? Everything go okay?" Before Goliath could reply, he continued with obvious pride in his voice, "Did you wow them with your mad police skills?"

"It went just fine," Goliath replied. With a laugh, he told him, "And it was a quiet week, so I didn't really have a chance to show off any mad skills."

"Well, there's always next week," Barton stated with certainty. "A small town can't be quiet all the time."

Reaching his truck, Goliath chuckled. "Well, one can hope."

After dealing with the crime in the city, Goliath wouldn't mind a little peace and quiet. He also hadn't shared his first day's *faux pas* with him, either. Goliath had no desire to explain his name hang-up to his father, seeing as his mother had chosen the name, and she was now deceased.

*Won't say a wrong word about my momma, no matter how much I question her decision.*

Goliath relaxed behind the wheel of his pick-up and chatted with his father for several minutes.

"Once you get that spare room set up," Barton told him as their conversation was winding down. "Let me know. I'd love to come out and see the place where my baby boy ended up."

Smirking, Goliath bit back a scoff.

*Baby boy.*

While Goliath lived up to his name, standing at six-foot-eight with a thickly muscled build to match, his father barely reached six feet. From what he understood, he'd inherited his size from his mother's side of the family. His grandfather had stood six-foot-seven, but he'd passed when Goliath was six, and he didn't remember him much.

"That sounds good, Dad," Goliath told the man. He didn't mention that his home was already set up. He had spent every evening that week putting his three-bedroom, two-bath home to rights. Goliath liked everything neat and tidy, and the boxes would have driven him nuts, even after just a few days. "Give me a few weeks to get a feel for the town. Then I'd love to have you out."

That would also give Goliath time to figure out just how accepting the town was to a man of his dimensions. He'd found that, sometimes, his size scared women and children. There had also been plenty of cases where men decided they needed to pick a fight with him . . . just because of his size. No way did Goliath want his father to pick up on that and get offended . . . or answer an asshole's desire for a fight.

*Don't need my fifty-five-year-old father trying to defend my honor.*

Then there was also the fact that as soon as Barton hit town, he would probably start scouring the area for a wife or husband for Goliath. Both his parents had been accepting when he'd admitted to asking boys out on dates just as often as girls while in high school. They hadn't cared one wit about the sex of his partner, as long as he was happy and cared for by his partner. So far, Goliath hadn't found *the one*, but he continued to hope.

*God, how embarrassing would it be to have my dad trying to set me up with every single man and woman he could find?*

Still, Goliath appreciated the sentiment even if he didn't need the action.

"Sure, son," Barton replied. "Stay safe out there."

"I will, Dad," Goliath assured. "Thanks."

After hanging up, Goliath started his truck, then pulled on his seatbelt. He glanced around the area before putting his vehicle into gear. Then he headed on home.

After a shower and change of clothes, Goliath stood in front of the open door of his refrigerator and grimaced.

"Right," he muttered. "Was supposed to stop at the grocery store on my way home."

Goliath thought about frying up his last half dozen eggs, but then he realized that he wouldn't have anything for breakfast. With a sigh, he closed the door before heading to his room. He grabbed a pair of socks and pulled them on, then moved to the front door for his boots and jacket.

After grabbing his keys off the rack near the door, Goliath headed out to his truck. He'd just slid behind the wheel when his stomach grumbled. He sighed as he started the vehicle.

He hated shopping on an empty stomach.

As Goliath pointed his truck toward Stone Ridge, he recalled Anthony and Markus's assessment of the town's restaurants. He'd already talked to Nathan, and his fellow deputy had agreed to meet him for a beer at *Spiron's* the following evening. Goliath decided to check out *Caribou's*.

"I could use a good steak," Goliath decided. "Then I won't be hungry when I shop afterward."

With that plan in mind, Goliath smiled. He turned onto Main Street and started checking out the signs on either side. He vaguely recalled seeing the sign, and he hoped he could find it again without difficulty.

A moment later, Goliath spotted it. He found a parking spot at the back of a small lot and turned off his truck. Sliding his keys into his pocket, Goliath shut his door as he glanced around.

Goliath thought the place looked pretty busy.

*Right. Friday night.*

*Hope there isn't too much of a line.*

Heading into the restaurant, Goliath glanced around, feeling relief to see there was only one couple waiting—a pair of men. When the blond glanced over his shoulder at him, he noticed how the small man's eyes widened as he looked him up and down. As if reacting to the blond, the broad-shouldered black man, who had his arm around him, peered at Goliath, too. That man's gray eyes narrowed just a smidge.

Goliath offered the pair a small smile, hoping to help them

relax.

The dark-skinned man turned fully. "Ye're Goliath Dick-man, aren't ye?" Without waiting for a reply, he offered a hand. "I'm Declan McIntire, the area's head park ranger."

"Oh, yeah. Hi. Nice to meet you." Goliath took Declan's hand and shook, recalling the sheriff mentioning the names of not only the head park ranger but several others as well. "Please, call me Ollie."

"As ye wish, Ollie." After releasing Goliath, Declan indicated the small blond man he had his arm around. "This is my husband, Doctor Lark Trystan." Declan jutted his chin toward Goliath and told his partner, "Ollie is Stone Ridge's newest deputy. He just started on Monday."

Goliath censored his strength as he shook the little guy's hand. "Nice to meet you, too."

Lark grinned broadly. "Back atcha." His blue eyes twinkled as he peered up at him. "Welcome to Stone Ridge."

"Thank you." Goliath appreciated the pair's friendliness.

"Hey, Declan," a woman called from the hostess stand. "Your table is ready." She grinned widely as she picked up a couple of menus. "Date night, huh?"

"Indeed it is, Talia," Declan confirmed, smiling at the woman. As they began moving toward her, Declan peered over his shoulder and offered, "I'm certain I'll be seein' ye again soon." With a wry smile, Declan added, "In these forests, our duties overlap often."

As Goliath nodded, he watched the pair walk away. Declan tipped his head down, murmuring to his husband. Goliath bet he was explaining who he was to the other man.

*A doctor. Damn.*

The hostess—Talia—returned and peered up at him. Her smile appeared a little reserved, but at least it was there. "Hi. Just you tonight? Or are you waiting for someone?" As Talia spoke, she picked up a menu.

"Just me," Goliath confirmed, offering a smile of his own.

Talia nodded. "I think one of our bistro-style tables would be the most comfortable for you," she offered as she began moving to the right. "Is that okay with you?" After another glance at him, Talia added, "If you're willing to wait a few minutes, one of our corner booths should open up soon. That'd be comfortable, too."

Goliath had been working around standard accommodations and his large size for years, and he had to smile upon hearing her trying to help him out.

"The bistro table will be just fine," Goliath told her. "Thanks."

With a grin, Talia took him to the table near the center rear of the restaurant. "Here you are, sir." As she placed the menu on the table, she asked, "Did I hear Declan right when he said you're our newest deputy?"

Goliath nodded. "Yes, ma'am."

Talia giggled as she beamed at him. "So polite." Then she touched his forearm, saying, "Welcome to Stone Ridge, Deputy." As Talia backed up a step, she told him, "Earl will be your server tonight. Don't forget to tell him you're our deputy." Talia turned back toward the front. "We give those in public service a discount."

As Talia headed back to her station, Goliath grunted softly and picked up his menu.

*Huh. How about that.*

Goliath had only been perusing the menu for a moment when a shadow fell over his table.

"Good evening, sir," a melodious tenor greeted. "I'm Earl, and I'll be your server tonight. Our specials for tonight are—"

There was a slight huskiness to the man's voice that went straight to Goliath's balls, and he lost track of what Earl was saying. He looked up and nearly swallowed his tongue. The blond man standing at his table, dressed in black dress jeans and a pale-green polo, nearly made him swallow his tongue.

As Goliath met his waiter's brown eyes, he felt his mouth go dry.

*Oh damn. He's gorgeous.*

# CHAPTER TWO

Earl Raukus could barely get his standard waiter's spiel past his dry throat. Sweat popped out at his temples, and the hairs on his nape stood on end. His hands trembled, and he gripped his pen and order pad tighter in an attempt to steady them.

*My mate is sitting right in front of me . . . and oh, gods! He's huge and gorgeous and drool-worthy and . . . shit, Earl! Get it together!*

At the age of sixty-seven, Earl was considered young for a wolf shifter. Having watched so many of his fellow wolf shifters find their mates, he'd longed for the day he would find his own. He certainly hadn't expected it so soon in his life, though.

Staring at the huge human sitting at the bistro-style table before him, Earl couldn't wait to learn everything about the handsome man. He longed to stroke the human's beautiful, smooth, lightly-tanned skin. Earl wondered how dark his chocolate-brown eyes would deepen to when in passion.

"I'll, uh—" The man paused and cleared his throat. "Uh, what beer do you have on tap?"

Between the man's slightly gruff voice as well as the pleasant perfume of masculine arousal beginning to flood the air, Earl knew his human was just as affected by him. He did a mental happy dance as he licked his lower lip. Earl noticed the way the guy zeroed in on the movement, making it difficult to answer, but he managed it.

After his mate made his choice, Earl didn't want to leave

right away. "Can I get an appetizer started for you?" he offered. Unable to help himself, he leaned close and pointed at a couple of items on the list. "The loaded potato skins are absolutely delish, and the hot wings are finger-licking good."

*Gods, there's so much of this man I'd love to lick.*

The man's nostrils flared as he glanced at the menu, then focused his attention on Earl. "The loaded skins would be fantastic, Earl," he rumbled, his eyes beginning to darken with obvious desire. "Thank you."

Earl grinned widely, just staring for a few heartbeats. The moment stretched . . . until a fellow waiter, Emily, nudged him with an elbow as she passed. Blinking, Earl looked Emily's way, and she eyed him with wide eyes and lifted brows.

*Right. Openly eye-fucking the customers is bad.*

After clearing his throat, Earl smiled at his mate. "I'll be right back with your beer."

"Thanks," the man replied in his deep whiskey voice, causing a fresh wash of heat to rush through Earl's body.

*Just damn.*

Before Earl could get lost in his mate's eyes once more, he hurried away. He stopped at the electronic kiosk in the back and entered his mate's order. Then he glanced over his section to see if anyone was looking his way as if needing something.

Recalling that his mate wasn't the only one who wanted a beer—a guy at the table he'd stopped at before becoming entranced by his newest customer had wanted a refill—Earl headed toward the bar. He quickly poured not only his mate's beer, but also the other customer's. Unable to help himself, Earl glanced his human's way. A shiver of pleasure trickled through him when he saw the man look away, having been caught staring.

*Gods, I really need to figure out his name.*

Earl took a deep breath, trying to gather a little self-control. Then he headed back to his mate's table and dropped off his beer. With a smile, Earl told him, "I'll be right back to get your order."

Seeing the huge man's small smile and nod, Earl grinned and hurried to drop off the other beer. He did a quick sweep of his tables, noting a couple of requests. One woman wanted an extra cup of ranch dressing for her salad, while a man at a different table needed more barbeque sauce for his riblets.

Then Earl found himself back at his mate's table. When he took a breath, he nearly groaned upon taking in another deep whiff of the human's masculine goodness.

"Wow."

The man's brows shot up. "Wow?"

*Oops.*

Feeling his cheeks heat, Earl admitted, "Didn't mean to say that out loud." His human continued to stare at him questioningly, so Earl told him honestly, "Your smell. You smell really good."

"Just showered," he told him softly, a smile toying around his lips. "Maybe you like the shampoo or body wash I use."

*Definitely not.*

"Perhaps." Earl lifted his order pad, offering the man another smile. "Are you new in town or just passing through?"

*Gods, that would suck, but I'll track him down if that's the case.*

"New in town," the man told him. After a second, he held out his hand. "Ollie."

While Earl wanted so much more than a handshake, he would accept being able to touch his mate any way he could. He gripped Ollie's hand and squeezed lightly. Earl didn't release him right away, and to his pleasure, Ollie didn't seem in any hurry to let go, either.

"Very nice to meet you, Ollie. I'm Earl Raukus," Earl told him honestly. His attention fell to Ollie's full lips for a second before he managed to snap his attention back to his eyes. "I'm certain you'll like it here."

"I have a feeling I will," Ollie replied, giving him a smoldering look that caused Earl's nipples to bead.

*Just damn.*

Still holding Ollie's hand, Earl asked softly, "Have you decided what to order, Ollie?" When his mate remained silent, he nibbled his bottom lip for a second before finding his tongue once more. "Or did you have any questions?"

"I do have a question, Earl," Ollie told him. "Are—"

"Earl," Emily interrupted, glancing from their still-joined hands to their faces. "There's a woman at one of your tables asking about more ranch dressing."

"Oh, right." Earl fought back a wince. "I'll be right with her."

Emily didn't look convinced, but she moved on.

*Crap. I hope I don't get into trouble.*

Earl released Ollie and asked, "What can I answer for you?"

Ollie glanced over his shoulder, obviously taking in Emily's retreating figure. Returning his attention to Earl, he rubbed the back of his neck. "Are the steak fries thick or thin?"

Something told Earl that wasn't what Ollie had originally planned to ask, but Emily had totally ruined the moment.

*We'll have more together.*

"They're moderately thick, but the cooks do a great job of getting them to just the right amount of crispiness," Earl answered. "I enjoy them."

Ollie nodded. "I'll take your bottomless riblet basket." Then he offered Earl his menu. "Please add on a Caesar salad."

Earl nodded. "Happy to." He jotted down the information. "I'll bring extra barbeque sauce, too. It's delicious."

As Ollie nodded, Earl realized he didn't have any reason to linger. "I'll go check on your appetizer."

"Thanks, Earl," Ollie murmured.

After another heartbeat of staring into Ollie's eyes, Earl

managed to tear his attention away from his mate. He hustled to the back and input his human's order. Then he quickly grabbed the items his other patrons wanted. Noticing Ollie's order of potato skins were ready, too, he grabbed them as well.

Unfortunately, while dropping them off, Earl noticed another man's empty beer mug, so he couldn't linger. He confirmed that the customer wanted another dark lager. That man's dinner companion requested another glass of wine, too, so he hustled to the bar.

While there, Earl spotted his friend Ulrick seated on the other side of the bar. He hadn't known the man long, but he enjoyed his company. Ulrick had recently shown up in town searching for a group of military men who'd been experimented on and turned into cheetah shifters. As it had turned out, Ulrick had undergone similar experimentation, but he'd been bonded with a jaguar.

Earl's wolf loved running with the large jungle cat. The man still had gaps in his memory, but he was turning into a good friend. Wanting to share his good fortune with his new pal, Earl headed that way.

"Hey, Ulrick," Earl greeted with a smile. "You didn't end up in my section."

Ulrick focused on him, one hand still around his beer mug. "Friday night is ramping up. Didn't feel like waiting for a table." With a shrug, he added, "Figured I'd run into you while sitting here." While Earl nodded and grinned, Ulrick leaned forward a smidge while sniffing discreetly. His eyes narrowed, and he murmured, "You smell . . . buoyant."

Earl barked a laugh. "Buoyant. Damn, haven't heard that word in ages. It's so true, though." Resting his elbows on the bar, he leaned toward his friend and lowered his voice. "I met my mate. He's here. In my section." Earl couldn't keep his excitement out of his voice even as he whispered.

Ulrick's eyes widened a smidge while the corners of his lips curved into a small smile. That was about as much emotion as the serious black ops soldier ever showed. It told Earl exactly how surprised, as well as happy for him, his new friend was.

"That's fantastic, Earl," Ulrick murmured. Reaching out, he touched the back of Earl's hand. "Who is he?"

"The big guy sitting alone at one of the high tables," Earl told Ulrick. He couldn't help the way his expression softened as he thought of his sexy mate. "Gods, he's gorgeous. His name is Ollie, and he's new in town."

Ulrick's nearly black eyes appeared to soften just a smidge. "Smitten already."

Snorting, Earl straightened. "Smitten. Love your word usage, Ulrick." Then he sighed, still smiling. "But right again. Totally smitten."

"Good for you." Ulrick patted Earl's hand. "Get back to work. Emily's scowling at you."

Earl heaved a sigh even as he nodded. "She's been totally on my case tonight. I better get back at it." With a grimace, he admitted, "I do have people waiting."

"Talk to you later, Earl." Ulrick straightened on his stool as he turned his attention to Darryl, the bartender, who approached with a basket of hot wings. "You can tell me all about him later."

After a nod, Earl returned to work. He poured the needed drinks and took them to their customers. As he passed Ollie's table, he was disappointed the man was focused on the potato skins and didn't glance up at him. Earl figured it was for the best.

After getting drink orders from a newly seated couple at another table, Earl headed to the kitchen. He found Ollie's order ready and placed it on a platter. Then he poured the sodas the new table wanted, added an extra container of barbeque sauce to his tray, and headed back out.

Earl dropped off the drinks before approaching Ollie's table. Anticipation filled him, and his body practically vibrated with excitement. He appreciated that his black jeans were tight enough to hide his half-hard dick.

"Here we are, Ollie," Earl greeted with a smile. He placed the Caesar salad on the table first, gaining his mate's attention. Upon seeing the shuttered expression on the big man's tanned face, he froze for an instant. "Uh, and your bottomless riblets and fries." When Ollie still didn't smile back, Earl nearly forgot to add the barbeque sauce. He glanced at the tray, confusion filling him. "Uh, here's the barbeque sauce." As Earl tucked the tray under his arm, he asked, "Can I get you anything else?"

"No, I'm good," Ollie rumbled, returning his attention to the food. "Thanks."

Even though Ollie's dismissal was clear, Earl stood stock-still in shock.

*What the hell?*

Needing to try again, Earl glanced at Ollie's half-full beer and asked, "Need another beer?"

"No."

Unable to help himself, Earl couldn't keep the hurt look off his face. He quickly cleared it, knowing it wasn't the time or place. Earl couldn't figure out Ollie's shift in behavior, and he felt his wolf whine in the back of his mind.

When Ollie continued to ignore him, digging into his Caesar salad, Earl knew he needed to get moving.

Hell, he was at work, after all.

Earl swallowed hard as he turned away.

*I'll check on him later. Maybe he's just hungry.*

Except, the next time Earl stopped at Ollie's table, his food was gone, and instead of asking for seconds when Earl offered, he replied, "Just need the check."

Confused and hurt, Earl did as his mate bid. The human

was ready with his debit card, not even glancing at the total. Earl quickly ran it, noticing the name on it read Goliath P Dickman.

*Goliath Dickman. No wonder he wants to be called Ollie.*

With a shake of his head, Earl returned to the table. His mate was already standing, ready and waiting for the receipt.

*Damn, is he tall. Wow! I wanna climb his six-foot-eight body in the worst way.*

"Did everything taste okay?" Earl asked, needing just a little more contact with his mate, although, by then, he sort of felt like a glutton for punishment.

"Yeah," Ollie replied shortly as he signed the check. "Everything was delicious."

Unable to help himself, Earl found his attention focusing on Ollie's jeans-clad ass . . . and it was a thing of beauty.

Except, when Ollie straightened and glanced at him, the human furrowed his brows. He even glanced toward the bar area. His jaw tightened, and he turned away as he grabbed his jacket from the back of his chair.

Disappointed, Earl whispered, "Have a good night."

As Earl collected the check, absently noticing that he'd received a twenty-percent tip, he couldn't figure out what the hell had changed.

*Why did my mate clam up?*

"Earl, is everything okay?"

Turning, Earl found Alpha Declan standing near his shoulder. "Um." He couldn't seem to help how small his voice came out, and he struggled with how to explain to the alpha wolf shifter.

Declan rested his hand on Earl's shoulder and squeezed lightly. "I scented yer distress from halfway across the room," he murmured, his black brows furrowing. "What happened?" Declan glanced in the direction of the doors. "Something with our town's newest deputy?"

"Ollie's our town's newest deputy?" Earl murmured, heart

17

speeding up in his chest as he thought about his mate in uniform. "Damn."

"Aye," Declan confirmed, squeezing once more. "Did he say somethin' bigoted or something?"

"No," Earl quickly assured, shaking his head. "He . . . he's my mate." Even as Declan's features morphed into one of surprised happiness, Earl added softly, "But he stopped chatting with me after I brought him his meal. I don't know why."

Declan glanced toward the door again, his expression turning musing. "Hmmm. I'll talk to Anthony about him," he assured. "Get his read on him." Returning his attention to Earl, Declan urged, "Finish yer shift, then go for a run tomorrow with yer friends. Take a bit of time to relax." With a reassuring smile, his alpha told him, "We'll sort this out."

"Thank you, Alpha," Earl whispered, then winced, realizing what he'd said.

After another reassuring squeeze, Declan released him and headed back toward his table.

Doing as his alpha recommended, Earl returned to work, doing his best to ignore Emily's stares.

# CHAPTER THREE

Goliath stared at the ceiling in his workout room, counting softly as he finished his third repetition of bench presses. Once he'd set the bar back in the cradle, he blew out a slow, deep breath and allowed his eyes to slide closed. As soon as he was no longer focused on keeping the proper form to the exercise, Goliath's attention returned to the hot waiter from the prior evening – Earl.

Immediately, Goliath's blood began flowing south, and his prick started to thicken. He wondered what it would feel like to thread his fingers through Earl's thick, ear-length blond hair. Goliath wanted to cup the man's nape, dip his head, and seal his lips over the other man's.

*What would he taste like?*

Groaning, Goliath lifted his head before banging it once on the padded bench beneath him. "Damn it," he grumbled. "Why can't I get him out of my mind?"

At first, Goliath had thought the sexy man had been flirting with him. He'd reveled in the guy's apparent interest. Hell, he'd almost asked the guy out.

Then Goliath had noticed the way Earl had leaned toward the man on the other side of the bar. He'd laughed and flirted with him, too. Disappointment had slammed into Goliath when he'd realized that it was just Earl's personality.

Goliath had shut down his interest – or tried to – and had stopped responding to Earl's friendliness. After all, it didn't really mean anything.

*So why did I see hurt flash in Earl's pretty brown eyes? My response couldn't really have hurt his feelings . . . right?*

Except, Goliath couldn't seem to push aside the feeling that Earl had truly cared. He hadn't meant to hurt the waiter. Goliath just hadn't wanted to feel led on by the man.

"What if there was really something there?" Goliath muttered as he eased to a sitting position, then to his feet. He grabbed a hand towel from a nearby side table. As Goliath wiped the sweat from his bare chest and pits, he recalled Earl's look of confusion and hurt . . . and how he'd stuttered around a few words when he'd first arrived at the table. "God, did I screw up a possible good thing?

"And now you're debating with yourself," Goliath muttered, rolling his eyes. Deciding he needed to talk to Earl again, he mused, "Wonder if he's working tonight."

Except, Goliath really didn't want to wait that long.

"What did he say his last name was?" As Goliath stretched his arms over his head, then across his chest, he recalled their conversation. As a police officer, he was normally pretty good at retaining information, even when distracted . . . and Earl was one hell of a distraction. "Earl Raukus." Goliath smiled, pleased with himself. "Wonder if you're in the phone directory, Earl."

Goliath picked up his phone and sat back down on the workout bench. After a second of hesitation, he pulled up the search app he had access to through his job on the force. He entered Earl's name.

A second later, Goliath not only had Earl's phone number, but also his address and a wealth of other information about the man. He stared at Earl's driver's license photo. Lifting his free hand, he traced his finger along the curve of the man's jaw, then his lips.

Feeling his blood stir, Goliath reached down and palmed his thickening prick. He groaned softly as he teased his balls through the thin material of his workout shorts. Goliath stared at Earl's attractive features as he continued to play with himself.

Realizing what he did, Goliath growled softly. He peered at his tented shorts as he rubbed his thumb up and down his shaft. His erection throbbed in time with each beat of his heart, and he ached for more stimulus.

With a grunt, Goliath pushed to his feet. He stalked out of his workout room and down the hall. Entering his bedroom, he pulled the waist of his shorts forward and down, easing it over his hard shaft. Then Goliath pushed the fabric down, letting them fall from his body as he continued to move.

Goliath entered his bathroom and reached into the shower. A quick adjustment to the knob had the water flowing and at the temperature he wanted. Easing under the spray, he sighed deeply as he enjoyed the feel of it soothing the muscles of his shoulders, arms, and torso.

After a moment, Goliath grabbed his washcloth and body wash. He squirted some onto the cloth and lathered it up before rubbing it over his skin. Goliath cleaned quickly, his body urging him to get to the good part of his shower.

Unable to resist for long, Goliath wrapped the soapy cloth around his erection. He rested the forearm of his other arm against the tile wall. With a soft groan, he began jacking himself.

Allowing his eyelids to slide closed, Goliath imagined it was Earl's hot mouth wrapped around his dick. He would skim the pretty man's hair away from his face, allowing him to peer into his eyes. Goliath just knew Earl would look so happy on his knees servicing him.

In his mind's eye, Goliath saw Earl smile obscenely around his erection. There were drops of water on the man's lashes, making his pretty brown eyes glitter. Goliath saw warmth there, hot desire and need.

Groaning, Goliath picked up his hand's pace. He tightened

his hold. His balls felt heavy, swollen with the need to come.

His imaginary Earl tightened his lips as he began bobbing along Goliath's prick. Somehow, he managed to take his full eleven-inch, thick length. His hot mouth sucked hard, applying exquisite sensation to the over-sensitized skin of his hard shaft.

Goliath jacked himself a few more times, and his balls pulled tight. He grunted as his cock pulsed in his hand. A shudder rolled through him as his orgasm hit his system, making spots dance before his eyes as his senses reeled with pleasure.

With a low growl, Goliath continued to work himself, imagining it was Earl milking him with his mouth and hand. Heat warmed him from the inside out, even as he sprayed all over the tile wall. Resting his forehead against his hand, he panted harshly under the heat of the spray.

Peeling his eyelids open, Goliath stared at the shower wall. His cum was already being rinsed away, whisking away the evidence of his fantasy. He wondered what it would take to enjoy his images for real.

*Is it even possible?*

Goliath released his softening prick as he heaved a deep sigh.

*I want to find out.*

Deciding to drive by Earl's home, Goliath finished cleaning up. He figured he could scope the place out. Maybe he would spot Earl leaving the house to go shopping or something. He could pretend to bump into him.

Rolling his eyes, Goliath turned off the water. "Great," he muttered as he grabbed a towel and began drying himself. "One meeting, and I'm turning into a stalker."

Still, Goliath couldn't deny the chemistry he felt simmering between them. He had to make certain it wasn't all one-sided. If Earl turned him down, then he would know for sure.

With that thought in mind, Goliath quickly dressed in re-laxed jeans and a green t-shirt. He didn't want it to look like he was trying too hard. Besides, the shirt molded to his massive chest, showcasing his muscles nicely.

Out of habit, Goliath strapped on his ankle holster after pulling on a pair of hiking boots. He grabbed a jacket and headed to the front door. After shoving his phone in one pocket and his wallet in another, he grabbed his keys and left the house.

Goliath entered Earl's address into his truck's GPS. Once it pulled it up, he began following the directions. The route took him out of Stone Ridge, heading north in a direction he hadn't explored yet. From maps Goliath looked at, he knew many of the homes in the area backed to national forest land, and there were a lot of hiking trails mixed in.

Taking in the pines lining the road, Goliath rolled down his window and inhaled deeply. He admired the beautiful scenery while relishing the fresh, fragrant air. When he'd lived in Nashville, he'd always wanted to live closer to the Smokey Mountains nearby. He'd been excited to have the opportunity to finally realize that dream, even if it ended up being in a state halfway across the country.

The flash of sunlight off something metallic in the trees to his left caught Goliath's attention. He slowed his vehicle as he checked his map. Even though he spotted an overgrown, rut-ted dirt track to the left, there weren't any houses along this stretch. Plus, the nearest trailhead was a good mile away.

*Is someone camping illegally?*

The crack of a gunshot filled the air.

With his cop instincts on alert, Goliath pressed on the brakes. He found a location on the opposite side of the road and eased his truck to the side. Goliath had read up on the area's hunting regulations, but he couldn't remember every-thing. Still, he knew there was no target practice allowed in the area.

Once Goliath parked off to the side, he eased from his vehicle. He glanced both ways, then jogged across the road. Watching and listening, Goliath searched the trees around him for movement.

Goliath didn't spot anyone by the time he reached the dirt track. Easing along the path, he crept forward. He saw the metallic gleam once more, and after another couple of steps, he saw the front fender of an older model, dark-blue *Ford* . . . and there was no license plate.

Frowning, Goliath kept a few trees between himself and the vehicle as he rounded the quad-cab, long-bed vehicle. When he reached the rear of the truck, he didn't find a license plate there, either. His mind spun as he wondered if it was abandoned or if the owners were up to no good.

After hearing the gunshot, Goliath was leaning toward the latter.

Just as Goliath was contemplating crossing to the truck to peer inside, he heard the snap of branches and the low murmur of voices. He eased backward and crouched behind a branch. After a moment, Goliath spotted a pair of men, and his blood ran cold.

They were dragging a large tawny-colored wolf.

*Holy shit! I didn't even know there were wolves out here.*

Another thought hit him just as quickly.

*These guys are poachers.*

"Quick, John, grab the crate out of the back," the blond-haired man ordered. "We gotta get him in before he wakes up."

The black-haired man, John, nodded and hurried to the back of the truck. After lifting the window of the shell on the truck, then lowering the tailgate, he dragged a metal dog crate from the back. John carried it to the blond's side and opened the door.

"Grab his shoulders," the blond ordered.

John glared at his companion. "How come I gotta be near

his head?" he asked belligerently, crossing his arms over his chest. "Why don't you get near its teeth, Ben?"

The blond, Ben, sneered at John. "Pussy. He'll be out for at least another thirty minutes, and we gotta hurry back and help Larry and Will with the others."

"Whatever." John moved toward the wolf's tail. "You do it then."

Ben curled his lip, but he did it. He grabbed the wolf's ear and lifted it while dragging the cage forward. Once he had the animal's head inside the door, Ben gripped the beast's shoulders and heaved.

At the same time, John grabbed the base of the wolf's tail and one upper leg. Between the two, they managed to shove the wolf into the cage. After locking the cage, Ben led the way back into the woods.

"Shit," Goliath hissed, scowling.

Pulling out his phone, he quickly located the sheriff's number. Then he realized there was someone else who would probably respond quicker — Declan McIntire, the head ranger for the area. Goliath located that man's number and dialed.

After the second ring, the sound of Declan's Irish-accented voice came through the line, "This is Declan."

"Declan, this is Deputy Dickman, uh, Ollie," he murmured, keeping his voice low. "I've run across poachers in the woods."

"Deputy," Declan began. Just as quickly, he snarled, "Poachers? Where? How do ye know?"

Goliath quickly summed up spotting the flash of sun off the truck and stopping to check it out. After giving his location, he added, "I didn't even know there were wolves in these woods."

"Can ye take a picture of the animal in the crate and send it to me?" Declan asked, not bothering to comment on the fact that wolves were out there. "And possibly disable the truck?

My men and I are on our way."

"Yes, sir," Goliath quickly replied. "I'll see what I can do."

Then Goliath ended the call and lowered the phone before he began creeping forward once more. He listened carefully as he made his way to the crated wolf. After snapping a picture of the tawny-colored wolf, Goliath sent it to Declan.

Goliath rounded the vehicle, inspecting it, racking his brain for possible ways to disable it. He decided to go with the tried and true flat tire. Pulling his utility knife from his belt, he flipped out the blade.

Crossing to the front passenger tire, Goliath crouched beside it. He reached under the truck, getting low to the ground. Stabbing with force, he sank the blade into the thick tire, then yanked it free.

Immediately, the tell-tale hiss of escaping air reached his ears. He quickly rose just enough to peer through the windows. After a sweep of the trees, he rose a bit higher and looked into the cab, searching for something that might identify the perpetrators.

*Nada.*

To Goliath's relief, the tire deflated fairly quickly, and it was fully flat before he heard the snap of branches, heralding Ben and his buddies' approach. Returning to his hiding place, he watched as four men exited the forest. Each pair dragged another wolf. A brown-haired man had a large tranquilizer rifle slung over his shoulder. The final man had black hair and had a hand gun strapped to his thigh.

Goliath wondered if that meant the others were armed, too.

As Goliath watched, John and Ben dragged two more cages from the back. He saw them stuff a black wolf into one of them. Just as they began maneuvering the blond animal into the third, the black-haired guy noticed the flat tire.

"Damn it, Ben," he snarled. "Why didn't you tell me we had a flat tire?"

Ben's eyes widened, and he lifted his hands in placation.

"It wasn't like that when we were here a few minutes ago, Will. I swear."

Will's cruel-looking eyes narrowed as he stalked over to the tire. After inspecting it, he rose and panned his gaze over the area. He also pulled his gun from his holster.

"Eyes up, guys," Will ordered. "We have company." As the other men glanced around, Will continued, "John, change the tire."

John looked around fearfully, then quickly got to work.

"Larry, get the serum," Will ordered, his lip curling. "Ben, pull that half-caged wolf back out."

"What?" Ben squeaked as the guy with the tranquilizer rifle placed the weapon inside the cab and pulled out a hard-sided case.

"It'll wake it up," Larry warned as he opened the case.

"I know." Will's voice hardened. "I want it awake." Scowling at a still-frozen Ben, Will ordered again, "Drag it out."

Ben looked like he was about ready to piss himself. "You wanna wake it up? R-Really?"

"Yeah, *really*," Will snarled. "If one of 'ems out there watchin,' I want him, too." When Ben still stared at Will with wide eyes, the guy snapped, "Don't want him identifyin' us, moron."

Ben nodded like a bobble head as he began pulling the blond wolf the rest of the way out of the cage.

"This one a friend of yours?" Will called as Larry moved toward the wolf holding a syringe with who the hell knew what in it. Will pointed. "Shift him."

Larry knelt beside the wolf and stabbed it with the needle.

A second later, the animal shuddered and jerked.

Bile rose up the back of Goliath's throat upon watching the cruelty of the men before him. He'd never been able to understand how anyone could treat an animal that way. Goliath weighed his options as he palmed his own weapon and swept his gaze over the assholes, wondering if he could incapacitate all four men before becoming too injured.

The odds weren't great.

Then Goliath returned his attention to the wolf. Except, where the animal had lain, there was no longer a wolf. There was a man . . . a naked man.

When Will used a foot to roll the guy onto his back, Goliath barely held in his gasp of shock.

Where, a few seconds before, a blond wolf had lain, now lay an unconscious Earl Raukus.

*What the ever-loving fuck?*

# CHAPTER FOUR

Lying still, regulating his breathing, Earl fought the urge to groan. He ached in a way he couldn't place. His limbs tingled uncomfortably, and he wanted to scratch at his arms something fierce.

Instead, he cataloged what he could feel and hear.

Earl smelled the earth and pine and felt the grass under his body. With his last memories of running in wolf form with his friends, Rainy and Nedrick, he wasn't certain why he would have passed out while outside. Earl wasn't prone to napping in the buff in the sun.

Then Earl heard a voice he didn't recognize.

"He should be waking any second, Will."

"Good." There was a definite coldness filling the second man's voice. "Come on out," the guy — Will — hollered. Earl felt a boot rest against his upper arm. "Or I'm gonna shoot this fucker in the leg."

*What the fuck?*

Earl barely resisted snapping his eyes open to see what the hell was going on.

"Won't he shift back?" another man asked, sounding uncertain and fearful. "He could hurt us."

"The serum won't let him," the first man replied, sounding bored. "It'll take at least a day before it'll wear off, keeping him in his human form unless I administer the counter serum."

That was when it hit Earl.

*Hunters found us?*

Earl had been warned. The whole pack had been.

A few weeks prior, a couple of hunters had been invited into the area by a woman named Michelle. She'd been fired from her dispatch and receptionist position at the sheriff's station. The hunters had been her cousins, and she'd wanted them to help her retaliate against the *faggots* who'd taken over the sheriff's station.

Michelle hadn't known her cousins were shifter hunters, but a man named Moris had figured out what they were. Instead of targeting them for being gay, he'd gone after them for being shifters. After being caught, Moris had revealed that he'd sent an encoded missive to a colleague.

Alpha Declan had warned everyone to be vigilant . . . to stay careful and keep watch while not only out running but while in town.

Earl could only equate forgetting due to meeting his mate . . . and being half-ignored by him.

Even as Earl lay on the ground, nude and at the mercy of hunters, a stab of sadness washed through him.

When Earl felt the guy's boot applying pressure to his arm, essentially shaking him, his attention snapped back to where it needed to be.

"Wake up, monster," Will demanded, shaking him some more. "I can't wait to hear your screams when I shoot ya."

"Shooting him will decrease his value." That came from the man with the bored tone.

"They heal fast," Will countered. "By the time of the auction, he'll have mostly healed." With a scoff, he added in a low voice, "Besides, if we can get the other one to come out of hiding, that'll be even more money in our pockets."

*Okay. Not just hunters. These guys are selling shifters. But to whom?*

Earl had never heard of a black market for shifters.

"I said, wake up."

A second later, someone—Will, presumably—smacked

him across the face.

Earl snapped his eyelids open and stared into cold brown eyes. The man sneered at him as he straightened. He gave Earl a nasty smile, then glanced around the area before refocusing on Earl.

"Call to your friend," Will ordered. "Let him hear your voice."

"Don't turn yourself over to these guys," Earl hollered, holding Will's gaze. "Tell Alpha they're going to sell us at auction."

"Shut up," Will snapped. Lifting his boot from Earl's arm, he hauled back and kicked at him. "Abomination."

Earl rolled toward Will, wrapping his arms around the man's leg as he swung. While it still impacted his gut, there wasn't as much power behind it. When Will tried to yank his leg away, Earl took those few precious seconds to glance around the area.

Rainy and Nedrick were already in cages. While Rainy's had already been lifted in the back of the enclosed truck bed, Nedrick's cage was only a few feet from him on the ground. Neither of them were moving, and Earl prayed that they were still just asleep.

Earl also spotted a man crouched near the front tire, which was currently up on a jack. He could also see boots on the other side of the truck, too.

"Get off me, fucker," Will ordered, pulling at his foot again, which Earl ignored.

The cocking of a gun drew Earl's attention. He jerked his attention upward . . . and found himself staring down the barrel of a revolver. Slowly, Earl released his grip on Will's leg and eased to his back.

"Not so tough now, are ya?" Will chortled coldly.

"Let's just hurry up with the tire and get out of here," another man said from the left. "We don't even know if the shifter who punctured our tire is still out there."

"This asshole better hope another shifter is out there," Will declared. "Otherwise, he's gonna bleed for nothing." Then Will lifted his head and glanced around the area. "Hear that? You have to the count of three to get your furry ass out here before I put a bullet in this fucker's thigh. One!"

Earl tensed.

"Two!"

Closing his eyes, he waited for the impact and the resulting pain.

Just as Will started to say three, the crack of a gun echoed through the air. Except, Earl felt nothing.

Will screamed.

Earl snapped his eyes open and discovered the gun on the ground near his leg. Will clutched his forearm just above where blood oozed from a wound. A number of cusses issued by the other men spurred Earl into action.

Lifting his leg, Earl swept it up and over, slamming his heel into Will's hip in an arc kick. The howling man lost his balance and toppled, hitting his head on the truck's bumper on the way down. He collapsed, out cold.

The man who'd been changing the tire had opened the front door and leaped inside. The guy who'd been on the driver's side was crouching behind the vehicle. Another shot tore Earl's attention to the right just as a briefcase erupted in a shower of plastic. The man next to it stumbled backward.

Earl grabbed Will's gun while leaping to his feet. He lunged at the fleeing man, tackling him to the ground. Using the butt of the weapon, he slammed it against the human's head, rendering him unconscious.

Feeling the sting of a bullet grazing his arm, Earl lunged left and rolled. He regained his feet and pivoted, intending to fire toward the truck. Spotting an open front door and the backsides of two fleeing men, he paused.

When one of them aimed awkwardly behind him, Earl sprinted toward the far side of the truck for cover. Except, the bullet pinged off the cage on the ground. Cursing under his breath, Earl realized the douche was aiming at Nedrick.

The report of a gun behind him made him cringe, but he chose to trust whoever was helping him. He didn't know who it was, but considering there were a whole lot of ex-military men in their pack, he had faith they knew what they were doing. The next time he heard the gun go off behind him, Earl lunged forward and grabbed the edge of Nedrick's cage. He hauled it toward himself and tucked it against the rear tire.

Seeing a bloom of blood on Nedrick's haunch, Earl winced. "Damn. So sorry, buddy," he whispered, hoping his friend would be okay.

Relief filled him when Earl saw the steady rise and fall of his side, telling him Nedrick continued to breathe. He wished he could pull his buddy out and assess him. Unfortunately, he continued to hear intermittent shots from the woods on the other side of the truck, although the weapon behind him had fallen silent.

After a few minutes, the sound of shots from the other side of the truck ceased, too.

"Earl? You and your help okay?"

Eyes widening, Earl called, "Ulrick?"

"Yup." Ulrick's growl came through the clearing. "These bastards are down." After a second, he added, "You with the gun. Identify yourself."

Earl slowly rose as he peered over his shoulder. Hearing the deep voice that responded, he couldn't help the way his jaw sagged.

"Ulrick a friend, Earl?"

"Ollie?" Earl gasped, shock thrumming through him.

"Yes."

Earl swallowed hard as he felt his blood flow south. His

prick began to thicken. Gritting his teeth, he did his best to remember why popping wood right then was an absolutely horrible idea.

"Earl?" Ollie called again.

Getting over his shock, Earl assured, "Yeah. Ulrick's a friend." As he watched, anticipation rising, he saw a hulking figure separate from the trees. As his mate drew closer, Earl clenched and released the muscles in his thighs, fighting his urge to run to the human. Earl couldn't help how he reverently whispered his mate's name. "Ollie."

Ollie paused at the edge of the small clearing holding the truck. After slowly sweeping his gaze over the area, his attention fixed on Earl. His eyes narrowed, and Earl finally understood the phrase, eating him up with his eyes.

Earl's heart thudded wildly, relief and pleasure swirling within him upon seeing the hungry desire flooding the man's dark eyes.

Then Ollie bent and lifted his pant leg. He slid his weapon into a holster hidden beneath. As he straightened, he whipped his shirt over his head, revealing his massive, ripped torso.

Earl nearly swallowed his tongue as he took in all his smooth, nicely tanned skin. Upon that view, there was no way to help how swiftly his blood flowed south. He could only stare . . . and pant, gazing with wide-eyed appreciation . . . as Ollie approached.

"Here," Ollie rumbled, holding out his shirt. His gaze flicked down, and he licked his lips. His voice came out husky as he murmured, "As much as I think that's a thing of beauty, you better put this on, Earl."

Earl took the offered item and pulled it over his head. The shirt was so large, it slipped to hang off one shoulder. The hem even reached mid-thigh, covering him effectively.

Still, Earl had to take a moment to bring the collar to his

nose. He inhaled deeply. Humming, he closed his eyes and relished the heady fragrance of his mate.

The fact that his mate's scent covered his body settled something within him. He would have equated it with his wolf, but he could barely feel the animal. As odd as it felt to be without him, he knew it was temporary.

"Earl? You okay?"

Earl snapped his eyelids open and met Ollie's gaze. Peering up the over half a foot height distance, he smiled tentatively at the man. Then he noticed Ollie's gaze focused on his right upper arm.

"Yeah," Earl assured, glancing at the graze from the bullet. It had already scabbed over, the blood that had dripped down his arm dry and flaking off his skin. "It'll be gone in a few days." Realizing what he'd admitted, Earl snapped his attention back to Ollie's face. "Um, I mean —" Glancing around, Earl truly had no idea how to explain . . . any of this. "Um."

Ollie rubbed the back of his neck, his brows furrowing. He took another look around, too, before returning his gaze to Earl.

"I sure as hell have a lot of questions," Ollie told him. "You gonna be able to answer them?"

Earl nodded. "I'll explain everything."

After all, Ollie needed to know anyway.

"Well, explanations can wait," Ulrick cut in, entering the clearing. He was dragging the pair of men that had fled, one by each leg. "You got a phone, Ollie? We need to call Declan."

Ulrick was also nude.

Earl growled softly under his breath, a wave of annoyance surging through him. For the first time in his life, he hated the fact that a shifter had to get naked to change form. As ridiculous as it was, Earl cast about for something for Ulrick to wear.

Spotting a sweatshirt in the back seat of the truck, Earl grabbed it and tossed it to his buddy. "Wrap that around your waist," he ordered, frowning.

Ulrick caught it. Arching a brow, he stared at Earl for one heartbeat, then two. His gaze flicked to Ollie for an instant before he heaved a put-upon sigh and did as Earl had requested.

"Yeah, I have a phone," Ollie replied.

Earl noticed his mate was looking at everything in the clearing except for Ulrick until he'd covered his bits.

"But I've already talked to him," Ollie revealed, resting his hands on his hips. "He's on his way with his people."

Reaching into the truck, Ulrick asked, "Why would you call Declan?" He grabbed a bundle of cloth and shook it out, revealing a shirt. Instead of pulling it on, he pointed at Ollie's utility knife. "Toss me your knife, would ya?"

Without question, Ollie obeyed, and Ulrick began using it to cut the shirt into strips.

"I saw John and Ben drag out the tawny wolf," Ollie revealed, taking one of the strips and crossing to the downed Will. "Since he's the head park ranger around here and this is the national forest, I called him about poachers."

Instead of joining him, Ulrick stopped at the caged Nedrick and opened the crate.

Earl felt like an idiot — *just standing around staring, right* — and quickly helped Ulrick ease his friend from the cage. As he began helping Ulrick inspect the wolf's wound, he had to ask, "Not that I'm not really glad to see you, Ulrick, but what are you doing here?"

Ulrick flicked a glance his way as he eased the fur away from the wound. "I heard you were out running, so I thought I'd join you. Was following your trail to catch up when I heard the gunshots."

"Why are you naked?" Ollie asked, frowning.

Turning his attention to Ollie, Ulrick replied, "I was running as my jaguar."

Ollie sighed deeply. After he'd finished tying the strip of fabric over Will's wounded arm, he rested one forearm on his upturned thigh. He used a finger to swirl it in their direction.

"Yeah, you're gonna have to explain all . . . that."

*Gods, my mate seems so calm. I hope explanations go well.*

# CHAPTER FIVE

*I was running as my jaguar.*

*What the hell does that even mean? Could it be similar to how one second there was a wolf on the ground, and in the next, it was a naked Earl?*

Goliath still wasn't actually entirely certain he believed what he'd seen. Admittedly, when he was a young man, he'd thought urban legends and myths were cool. Never once did he believe that any of them were true.

"We should really call Declan first," Ulrick insisted, glancing his way with narrowed eyes. "He needs an update, at the very least."

Nodding, Goliath pulled out his phone and dialed Declan.

This time, the man answered on the first ring. "Ye have an update?" he asked in lieu of a greeting.

"Yes, sir," Goliath replied and quickly filled him in. "One of the wolves was shot."

"Nedrick," Earl offered, giving the animal a name. After a second of hesitation, he told him, "Rainy is still in a cage, but he's safe now."

Once Goliath repeated it, Declan growled softly. "Lark, call Travis," he stated, obviously not talking to Goliath. Then he must have returned his attention to their call, for he stated, "And how are ye holding up, Ollie? Staying calm?"

"So far, but I have a hell of a lot of questions," Goliath replied honestly. After a second of hesitation, he added, "Are you one, too?"

"Aye, Ollie," Declan replied without asking for clarification. "And we'll explain everything. We're just a few minutes out. Ah, scratch that. I see yer truck. See ye in a minute."

"Okay."

Goliath glanced at the phone and saw the line had been cut. A noise off to the side caught his attention, and he noticed one of the men Ulrick had dragged out of the woods beginning to stir. Hurrying over to him, Goliath pulled off his belt as he moved. He quickly grabbed the man's arms and tied them behind his back.

By the time Goliath had finished, the man — John, if he remembered correctly — had begun to struggle. "Hey, what are you doing?" He craned his neck to look over his shoulder at him . . . and his eyes widened as big as saucers. His words came out in a whisper. "What the hell? A-Are you a bear shifter?"

Scowling at the man, Goliath shook his head. "No. I'm human."

*Damn. What a weird thing to have to claim.*

John glanced around, his attention taking in his fallen companions before snagging on the mostly nude men working on the wolf. Snapping his attention back to Goliath, John hissed, "Why are you helping the monsters?" He glanced toward Earl and Ulrick again before adding, "Get me loose and help me take 'em. I can make ya rich, man."

Goliath rolled his eyes. "Asshole." Rising, he ignored the man's continued urging in favor of raiding the truck for supplies to tie up the others. Once that was done, he crossed to Earl. After a second of hesitation, Goliath lowered to one knee and asked, "How is he?"

Considering the name, Goliath assumed it was a he.

"Let's just say I'm glad whatever they shot him with is keeping him asleep," Ulrick stated coldly, shaking his head as he kept pressure on the wound. When Goliath gave the man a questioning look, the dark-haired man told him, "It's really better for the bullet to be removed before he shifts."

Goliath blew out a breath as he rocked back onto his ass. Crossing his legs, he rested his forearms on his thighs. He felt so out of his depth.

"So, John called you a shifter," Goliath began slowly, even as he heard the footsteps of others approaching. He turned his head and spotted Declan, Lark, and a number of others appearing between the trees. As Goliath watched them, he mused, "Is that what you call yourselves?"

"It is." It was Declan who answered, stopping next to him. Although, he didn't look at Goliath, as he was too busy surveying the area. "We are one of many paranormal species that exist right alongside humans." Finally, Declan looked down and met his gaze. "We live in secret, and pretty much just want to live our lives in peace like everyone else."

Goliath blew out a breath as he nodded slowly. He glanced at the trussed men on the ground. "They were going to sell them," he murmured softly, shaking his head. "Why would they want to sell one of you?"

"Because they're assholes," Lark muttered from where he knelt beside Nedrick. "Bigoted assholes."

Declan rested his hand on Lark's shoulder, perhaps to offer comfort.

Sitting, Goliath watched as a number of men carried the unconscious men away. Another hauled a bucking, snarling John to his feet and forced him to follow them. Still more pulled the black wolf from the cage in the bed of the truck while others searched the pick-up truck.

"Got a VIN number," a lean, toned man stated. "Gonna check it out."

"Sounds good, Prier. Keep me updated," Declan stated with a nod. He focused on a broad-shouldered Native American and ordered, "Kajika, when will Travis arrive?"

"He's ten minutes out," Kajika replied as he handed another man a tool to finish changing the tire.

Declan touched Goliath's shoulder, drawing his attention. "Ye haven't started asking questions yet, Ollie," he murmured, his expression one of concern. "Are ye in shock?"

Goliath startled upon feeling someone take his hand. Peering left, he realized Earl sat next to him on the ground. The pretty man eyed him with clear concern in his brown eyes.

"Uh, perhaps," Goliath admitted, liking the feel of Earl's hand within his own. He couldn't remember the last time he'd done something as simple as hold anyone's hand. Maybe his mother before she passed. Squeezing Earl's fingers lightly, Goliath asked, "Not that I'm minding, but why?"

"To make you feel better," Earl told him softly. With a small smile curving his lips, he added, "Because I want to. Want to touch you."

Glancing toward Ulrick, who'd moved off to help another man clean up the area, Goliath tipped his chin toward the man. At some point, someone had given the guy a pair of sweatpants, a shirt, and some sneakers. With him dressed, Goliath had studied him a little, and he'd realized that was the man at the restaurant.

"Won't your boyfriend care?" Goliath asked, unable to keep the gruffness from his voice. The surge of jealousy rushed through him, fast and hard, and he had to look away from the other man. Goliath stared at their joined hands, instead, wondering if he should pull away.

Earl squeezed his hand, so Goliath lifted his focus to the man's face. "I don't have a boyfriend."

Narrowing his eyes, Goliath countered, "I saw you at the restaurant last night." Disappointment filled him upon discovering that Earl was a liar. "He visited you at the bar. Touched your hand. You had your heads together." Goliath couldn't help the way his voice grew gruffer the more he spoke. "It was intimate, Earl."

With wide eyes, Earl whispered, "That's why you backed off." He shook his head once, looking as if he'd just figured something out. "You thought I was with Ulrick and was just being a friendly waiter."

Goliath grunted in confirmation.

Earl quickly shook his head, squeezing Goliath's hand tighter. "I don't have a boyfriend," he repeated. "I've never had a boyfriend. Shifters don't normally enter a relationship until"—he paused for a second, nibbling his lower lip, before he finished—"well, until we meet our mate."

"Your mate?" Goliath repeated softly. He didn't know what that meant, but he got the gist that Earl didn't do relationships. *Damn.* "So, uh, you just . . . do one-night stands?"

Goliath wondered if once would be enough with the sexy man. As he thought that, he realized that it didn't even matter to him that the man could turn into a wolf. Well, he would have to confirm that the man wasn't going to change during sex or maybe keep away from him during a full moon.

*Wait. It's daytime, and he was a wolf.*

*Okay. That's another weird thought.*

"For the most part, that's true," Earl confirmed, refocusing Goliath on the conversation. The man shrugged. "Or friends with benefits."

*Hmmm . . . I wonder if that would work for us.*

"I think ye're giving Ollie the wrong impression, Earl," Declan chided gently, shaking his head. "What Earl is trying to tell ye is that *you* are Earl's mate."

"Uhhhh, but I'm not a shifter." For the second time in an hour, Goliath pointed out, "I'm a human."

*Still feels weird to say.*

"A mate can be any species," Declan told him with a smile. "A mate is the other half of a shifter's soul. Someone they connect with on a soul-deep level, can build a relationship with, and bond with." Pointing at Lark, Declan told him, "Lark is my mate, and he's a human." Glancing around the area, he added, "Many of my wolves have found their mate in a human. Others have found them in other shifters, a few vampires, and even a gargoyle, although he lives with a clutch now."

Blinking, Goliath felt his brain begin to shut down.

*Vampires. Gargoyles. Clutch.*

*What the fuck?*

Goliath's pulse sped up, and he rubbed his free hand over his jeans-clad thigh. Shaking his head once, he frowned at the ground. He even squeezed Earl's hand tighter, as if the contact could ground him.

Declan sighed deeply. "Sorry, Ollie. I seem to have overloaded ye." He gripped his shoulder and squeezed lightly. "Why don't ye give yer keys to Earl. He can drive ye to his place. Ye can sit, relax, decompress." With a smile, Declan added, "Because ye're mates, his presence will help ye relax and process. Plus, he can answer any questions ye have."

"I kinda feel like I'm dreaming. Except, I don't have this kind of imagination." Goliath blew out a harsh breath as he looked up at Declan. "I'm assuming you'll need me to swear to secrecy. I'm not going to tell anyone," he assured.

"I didn't think ye would." Declan took a step backward and held out a hand to him, palm up. "But it'd be best if ye weren't alone right now. Bein' in shock and all."

Goliath nodded slowly, figuring that made sense. "Okay." Taking Declan's hand, he accepted the man's help in rising to his feet. "Damn. You're stronger than you look," he murmured when the smaller male had no trouble assisting him.

Declan smiled up at him. "Shifters have increased strength, speed, senses, and a few other perks." With a sigh, he sobered. "There is much ye'll learn over the next few days as ye adjust to yer new normal."

As Goliath nodded, he dug his keys out of his pocket. Handing them to Earl, he finally noticed the blond had donned sweats and sneakers given to him by someone. For some reason, Goliath really liked that the man still wore his shirt.

Pushing aside the odd rush of possessiveness, Goliath glanced around uneasily. "So, uh." He waved his hand to indicate the area still crawling with men—shifters. "What's going to happen with this? Are you reporting them to Sheriff Anthony? I guess I'll need to file a report." Goliath frowned. "Not certain how to write up something like this."

"No. When ye're ready, ye'll be giving a verbal report to me and a few others in the pack," Declan told him, surprising him. "This doesn't go through human channels." Then he smirked as he added, "Although Sheriff Anthony will know about it. He's part of my pack."

Goliath couldn't help the way his brows shot up. "He's a wolf shifter, too?" He shook his head slowly. "How many of you guys are out there?"

"In this area, there are over a hundred, but not all of them are wolf shifters," Declan revealed. "And Anthony is a poison dart frog shifter."

"Poison dart frog," Goliath repeated on a whisper, searching his mind for what that would be. The image of a colorful tree frog from the jungle popped into his head. "Oh, wow." Then Goliath frowned, refocusing on Declan. "I guess that's why John asked me if I was a bear shifter. Do you have those around?"

"There's a polar bear shifter who visits the area to stretch his legs on occasion. His name is Brad," Declan told him as his brows furrowed. "Which one is John? Do ye know them from somewhere?"

"No, I'd never seen them before," Goliath told him with a shake of his head. "I watched and listened long enough to catch all their names. John was the one awake. Will was the guy shot. Larry was the man over there." Goliath pointed.

"He was the one with the tranquilizer rifle and the darts that put your guys to sleep." His gaze strayed to Earl. "He was also the one who jabbed Earl with something that made him turn into a man. He said that Earl wouldn't be able to shift back to a wolf for at least a day." Thinking about that, Goliath waved a hand at the sky. "It's daytime, so I assume you don't need a full moon. Does that mean you can usually turn into an animal whenever you want?"

"Yeah, we usually have total control over it," Earl claimed, his voice soft. "Not being able to feel my wolf is really disconcerting."

"Huh." Goliath didn't know what else to say to that.

"I'll send Manon over to draw yer blood, Earl," Declan told him. "After he's done taking care of" —he glanced Goliath's way—"Will, ye called him?"

Goliath nodded.

"The fact that he knows there are other shifters in the area is troubling," Declan mused, crossing his arms over his chest. "We'll get to the bottom of this group of hunters, though. We always do."

When Earl took Goliath's hand and began leading him away, he glanced back at Declan. The man continued to stand over Lark, who appeared to be sewing up the wolf's wound.

As Goliath allowed Earl to guide him to his truck, he wasn't entirely certain he wanted to know what the man meant by that.

# CHAPTER SIX

*My poor mate. He's totally in shock.*

Earl had thought Ollie was processing everything well. Then the real explanations had begun, and he'd sort of just shut down. Once Declan had mentioned vampires and gargoyles, his mate had just sort of . . . checked out for a while.

Deciding a change of topic might be helpful, Earl asked, "So, what were you doing out here?" He glanced his mate's way, taking in the relaxed jeans he wore. "Checking out hiking trails or something?"

"Uh, was coming to drive by your house, actually," Ollie admitted. Once again, he rubbed his palms over his thighs, drawing Earl's attention to their massive thickness.

*Just wow. Wait. What did he say?*

Earl glanced Ollie's way before returning his attention to the road. "You were coming to see me?" Pleasure filled Earl, and he couldn't help but grin.

Ollie nodded slowly. "Well, I was going to look for you, at least." After clearing his throat, he admitted, "I don't know if I would have had the courage to stop and knock on your door."

Realizing he'd forgotten something important, Earl reached over and rested his hand over Ollie's on his thigh. "Thank you," he murmured, squeezing his mate's large hand. "For rescuing me."

With half his attention on the road and the rest on Ollie, Earl saw his mate turn his attention to him. "I was trying to figure out how to stop them before I knew it was you." His brows furrowed as his expression turned vacant. "Then there you were. Naked. Lying on the ground where the pretty wolf had been."

Ollie's deep voice softened even further, and if Earl hadn't been a shifter with heightened hearing, he wasn't certain he would have made out the words.

"Then that asshole stepped on you. He smacked you and kicked you." An angry growl erupted from Ollie. "And threatened you with a gun. I couldn't just sit and do nothing, but I knew surrendering to him would have been pointless."

"Again. Thank you."

Earl felt the words were inadequate, but at the moment, they were all he had.

Spotting his driveway, Earl slowed the large truck. He turned and headed up the gravel road. After he'd stopped before his closed garage, he put the truck in park and turned off the engine.

Squeezing Ollie's hand once more, Earl encouraged, "Come inside with me. We'll talk." He saw the way Ollie's dark eyebrows twitched, so he quickly added, "Or we'll just get a drink. Sit and relax." Then, unable to help himself, Earl murmured huskily, "Make out or fuck like bunnies."

Ollie sucked in a sharp breath and snapped his attention to Earl.

With a wink, Earl released his hand and exited the truck. He felt his dick twitch in his sweats. Just the thought of making out or fucking had him primed and ready.

*No, wait. My mate's scent, his presence, does that. Plus, he still isn't wearing a shirt.*

Earl led the way to his front door, and he couldn't help looking over his shoulder over and over again. He tracked his gaze over his mate's wide shoulders, defined pectorals, and six-pack abdominals. His mate's arms were thick with muscles.

As Earl opened his front door, he admitted, "I noticed your

real name on your debit card last night."

Ollie paused in the doorway, his eyes narrowing. "Okay."

Slipping his forefinger into Ollie's belt-loop, Earl tugged him forward a few steps so he could close the door. "Did you change your name to Goliath after you sprouted to six-foot-eight?" he asked curiously. "And how'd you get the nickname Ollie?"

Earl watched as Ollie's expression shut down. His jaw clenched. His eyes narrowed further. Even the muscles of his arms flexed as he clenched his hands into fists.

Not to mention, Earl noticed the way Ollie's scent darkened with . . . frustration and a hint of anger.

"Oh, damn," Earl whispered, cocking his head. "I've hit on something that upsets you." Taking a chance, he rested his palms on his mate's chest and began rubbing gently over his pectorals. After all, the touch of a mate was supposed to be soothing. Earl tipped his head back and peered into Ollie's upset features. "I'm so sorry, handsome. You don't have to tell me shit if you don't want to."

Slowly, Ollie's muscles relaxed beneath his ministrations. After a moment, he lifted his hands and settled them on Earl's upper arms. He didn't pull him closer, but he didn't push him away, either.

Standing that way for a moment, Ollie searched Earl's expression.

Earl didn't know what Ollie was looking for, but he must have found it. A small smile curved his lips for a few seconds. Then Ollie peered around the room slowly.

"Can I get some water, please?" Ollie muttered gruffly. "Then we can sit, and I'll explain."

Nodding eagerly, Earl eased a step backward. He took a second to skim his palms over and down his mate's arms. Then he started across his open-concept home.

Pointing to the right, Earl offered, "Please, have a seat on the sofa." He glanced at the empty hearth and couldn't help but ask, "Do you want me to start a fire?"

Earl opened a cupboard while watching Ollie move to the sofa and ease onto it. Over the sound of the water running as he filled two large glasses, he heard Ollie murmur, "No, you don't have to go through all that trouble."

After turning off the water, Earl rounded the kitchen bar that separated the living space from the kitchen. "It's no trouble." He handed the glass to Ollie as he admitted, "I like to start a fire nearly every night. I love to lie before it and enjoy the heat on my fur."

Ollie's lips twitched, and his expression blanked as he took a sip of water. Maybe he was imagining that. Then shrugged before shaking his head.

Meeting Earl's gaze, Ollie told him, "I need to leave in a couple of hours."

He glanced toward the clock on the wall. It depicted a nature scene — a river running through a forest to a valley with animals in various locations, including wolves howling at the full moon, a bear in the river trying to catch a jumping salmon, and a pair of deer drinking further downstream. The clock also told the time — almost half past two.

"I'm supposed to meet Nathan at *Spiron's* at six for a drink."

Earl almost spit out the gulp of water he'd just taken. Plopping down on the coffee table, he swallowed hard. He faced Ollie, coughed once, then frowned at his mate.

"You're going on a date with Nathan?" Earl snarled, anger surging through him. "Nathan Kaldwell your co-worker?"

For a second, Ollie's brows furrowed, and a look of confusion crossed his features. Then he smiled as he shook his head. His expression softened, and he just stared for a few heartbeats.

After taking another sip of water, Ollie told him, "No, I'm

not going on a date with Nathan." He scoffed as he told him, "I'm meeting a co-worker for a drink in order to apologize for being an ass on my first day of work on Monday." Sobering, Ollie told him, "It's part of the reason why I've been telling people to call me Ollie."

Earl blew out a long breath as his ire eased. Easing forward, he moved from the coffee table to the sofa, leaving his glass on the table. Sitting next to his mate, he couldn't resist the allure of all that skin. He rested his left hand on his human's shoulder while placing his other on his thigh.

"Will you tell me what happened?"

Ollie's shoulders lifted as he took a deep breath. After letting it out, he leaned forward and placed his glass beside Earl's. It was already nearly empty, attesting to how thirsty his mate had been.

Turning his head to focus on Earl, Ollie told him, "My mother named me Goliath. I really have no idea what she was thinking." He winced. "Goliath Dickman. I mean, really? It sounds like a porn name."

Earl would never say it out loud, but it kinda did.

"Uh, did she not want to have you or something?" Earl hazarded a guess. Wincing, he offered, "Or maybe the birthing drugs messed with her brain?"

"I actually asked, and Mom had a natural birth," Ollie told him. "I was named after her great-grandfather. I don't think she considered it in conjunction with our last name."

Fighting back a wince, Earl offered, "Oops?"

"Yeah." With a sigh, Ollie admitted, "It's gotten me into trouble a time or two. I don't have much of a temper." He cut a look Earl's way before lifting a hand and placing it over Earl's on his leg. "Until someone makes fun of my name. Momma gave me that name, and she's passed on now. When someone makes fun, I . . . I just see red." Ollie paused, his brows furrowing as his expression turned a little pained.

"And now I'm disrespecting her by asking people to call me Ollie." Turning his head, he met Earl's gaze. "Will you call me Goliath, please?"

Earl smiled as he squeezed Ollie's leg. *No, Goliath's leg.* "Of course, my mate."

"Thank you." Goliath squeezed Earl's hand back. "Anyway, Nathan teased me about my name first thing." His voice was soft, nearly a whisper. "I just snapped. I moved here to get away from the verbal abuse." With a roll of his eyes, Goliath added, "And the shit shifts given to me by a vindictive boss." He continued with a shake of his head. "To face it my first day, I . . . I had Nathan pinned to the wall with my hand around his throat. Nereo and Anthony pulled me off him."

Wincing, Earl murmured, "Damn. Sorry to hear that."

Then Goliath surprised Earl by asking, "Is Nereo a shifter, too? Declan said Anthony was, and he mentioned increased strength." He seemed to be rambling, as if he were mentally putting things together. "That would explain why the pair was able to pull me off of him. What about Nathan?"

"Nathan is human." After a second of hesitation, Earl admitted, "Nereo is a vampire."

"Vampire?" Goliath whispered, sucking in a sharp breath. "Oh." After swallowing so hard that his Adam's apple bobbed, he muttered, "But he's worked several day shifts, and he had pizza with us."

Earl chuckled softly. "Uh, most of the myths about vampires are total crap," he assured, sliding his fingertips along the top of Goliath's shoulder, tracing the tendon he longed to bite while claiming his mate. "They're not restricted to the night, and most think garlic is tasty."

His mouth watered just at the thought of biting his mate, but since he couldn't feel his wolf, he wasn't entirely certain he would be able to do it until that shitty serum wore off.

Goliath shivered under Earl's touch. "Oh." His brows furrowed. "Do they drink blood?"

"They do," Earl confirmed. Upon seeing Goliath's tension return, he quickly added, "But Nereo is bonded, so he would never approach you . . . or anyone, for that matter."

"Huh." Goliath cocked his head. "What's bonded?"

Appreciating the return to discussing their connection, Earl explained, "Well, a vampire has a soul mate just like shifters do. They call that person their beloved." He loved that his mate seemed to be focusing on him with rapt attention. "They bond with their beloved, just like a shifter mates with their . . . mate." Even as Earl winced at how poorly he'd worded that, he forged ahead. "When vampires and shifters find that special someone, he . . . or she . . . will spill their seed in their partner's body and give them a claiming bite. That will twine their life threads, allowing the human, if it is a human, to live as long as their paranormal partner will."

"How long is that?"

*Gods, we missed so much.*

"Uh, shifters live upward of five centuries," Earl explained. Upon seeing Goliath's brows shoot up, he hesitated. Then, knowing he should just lay it out there, Earl told him, "I'm considered quite young for a shifter to find his mate. I'm only sixty-seven, which means" — he swept his gaze over Goliath's face, taking in his big eyes — "uh, well, it means that barring something catastrophic, we could be together for another four hundred plus years."

"Damn," Goliath whispered, even as his brows furrowed. "That's a long time." Before Earl could come up with a response, he added, "How do shifters decide on mates? I mean, sure we have chemistry, I won't deny that, but we don't even know each other." Goliath sounded confused as hell. "You're claiming me as your mate, but how can you possibly know that you'll want me for four hundred years?"

Earl smiled as he skimmed his hand up to tease his fingertips along Goliath's neck. "I can't ever imagine not wanting you, Goliath," he whispered, wanting so very badly to urge his mate to turn his head so he could capture his mouth. "And while I would have been attracted to you regardless, Fate points out our mate to us. She heightens our awareness, increasing our attraction and need to touch, to taste, to just generally be with each other." Gliding his right hand up Goliath's thigh, Earl massaged the thick muscle. "I want to please you so very badly. I ache with it," he admitted. "Will you let me?"

Goliath's deep brown eyes smoldered as he gazed at Earl. His nostrils flared, and his chest heaved with each of his deep breaths. When Goliath slipped out his tongue, gliding it over his bottom lip, Earl couldn't help but stare at that glistening flesh that he wanted to taste so badly.

"I-I think—" Goliath began slowly, his voice rough. He swallowed so hard his Adam's apple bobbed.

The heady scent of Goliath's arousal perfumed the air, and Earl was having a hell of a time focusing. Still, he managed to whisper, "What do you think?"

Working his jaw for a second, Goliath seemed to be working through something in his mind. He blinked, his focus falling to Earl's lips.

"I think I'm about to let my dick do the thinkin.'"

In the next instant, Goliath turned toward Earl on the couch. He grabbed his hip with one hand while threading his fingers through his hair with the other. Then he leaned forward and slanted his mouth over Earl's.

Earl gripped Goliath's nape and opened to his mate. He immediately found himself full of his human's questing tongue. There was nothing tentative about Goliath's kiss as he mapped Earl's mouth.

His mate didn't ask.

He took.

He ravished.

Using his big body, Goliath pressed Earl backward, laying him over the sofa cushions.

Earl relaxed beneath the much larger man, more than happy to go along for the ride.

# CHAPTER SEVEN

Goliath couldn't remember the last time he'd been so hard for so long. His body felt primed in a way he'd never before experienced. The simple touches to his neck, the squeezes to his thigh, had sent his blood roaring through his veins, driving every semblance of coherent thought right out of his head.

As Goliath swirled his tongue around Earl's mouth, he groaned with pleasure at the other man's taste. He didn't know how someone could taste sweet and earthy at the same time, but Earl somehow pulled it off. His flavor reminded Goliath of a mixture of toffee and scotch.

*Mmmmm.*

As Goliath swirled his tongue around Earl's mouth, he felt the hairs on his nape stand on end. The skin of his arms goose bumped. A flush of heat rolled through his body, flaming him from the inside out.

Feeding Earl a groan, Goliath skimmed his hand down the side of his hip. He reached the hem of his shirt. Sliding his fingers under the fabric, he sought out the smooth skin he'd seen on display earlier that day.

All Goliath could think about was running his palms all over the other man's gorgeous flesh.

Earl arched beneath him, pressing into his touch. His one hand gripped Goliath's upper arm, clutching at him tightly. He scraped the nails of his other hand up and down his neck sensually, sending a cascade of tingles down his spine.

The sensations spread over his flesh, causing his nipples to bead. His gut clenched, and a shudder worked through him. As his cock throbbed, he groaned once more.

Needing pressure in the worst way, Goliath used the hold on Earl's hip to adjust Earl's hips on the cushion. He turned his body, rolling onto the man he soon planned to make his lover. With a knee, he pushed between the other man's thighs.

Goliath's need to breathe finally forced him to break the kiss. Lifting his head, he panted harshly as he took in the smaller man's features. He relished Earl's kiss-swollen lips, parted as he, too, struggled to get enough air into his lungs. His eyes were heavy-lidded as he peered up at him with hunger gleaming in his brown eyes.

Earl's borrowed shirt hung off one shoulder, exposing the slender line of his throat. Riveted at the sight of the smooth column, he lowered his head once more. He began placing sucking kisses down his jaw, and a fresh wave of heat swept through him when Earl tipped his head to the side, giving him more room to explore.

"So gorgeous," Goliath rumbled as he began placing sucking kisses over the sensitive skin of his Adam's apple. "Want to see, to feel, more of you."

With that thought in mind, Goliath forced himself to ease his hold. He levered up a bit. He put just enough space between them to allow him to grab his shirt. To Goliath's pleasure, as he tugged, Earl lifted his arms, allowing him to pull it easily from his body.

After dropping it off the side of the sofa, Goliath paused and stared. He took a moment to skim the backs of his fingers up Earl's side as he admired the other man's smooth, tanned flesh. Goliath tweaked one of the man's nipples, watching it bead. His new lover let out a breathy moan and arched into his touch, a shiver working through him.

"You're so responsive," Goliath stated on a moan. He scraped his nail over Earl's second nipple, making it tighten into a hard point. "Damn, you're sexy."

"Oh, gods, Goliath," Earl whispered harshly. He squeezed Goliath's upper arm and pulled. "Come here. Want to feel you."

Goliath sprawled over Earl, more than on board with that. Feeling the heat of his new lover's lean torso press against his own broader chest, he shuddered with delight. The scrape of Earl's fingernails along the sides of his back yanked a delighted hiss from him, and he tucked his head against the crook of Earl's neck as he pushed up into his touch.

That left a little space between their hips, and Earl seemed to take complete advantage. As Goliath lapped sucking kisses along the tendon where Earl's neck met his shoulder, he felt the other man turn his hands and palm his abdominals. Earl pushed his fingertips into the waistband of his pants, massaging the grooves of his hip.

With his cock jerking and throbbing, Goliath sucked in his stomach, offering Earl more room. His lover accepted the silent invitation. With one hand, he pushed his fingertips inside Goliath's underwear to massage the sensitive skin under his pubes. Earl deftly opened his fly with his other hand.

Goliath's eager erection pressed against the fabric of his boxer briefs, and he hissed a sigh of relief. Tipping his head, he rested it against his new lover's collarbone. He watched as Earl skimmed his fingers up his cloth-covered erection. At the same time, he continued to massage the groove of his groin.

His cock throbbed and twitched upon the light stimulation. He shuddered and gasped. Gritting his teeth, he clenched his hands, barely resisting the urge to press his hips against Earl's.

"Please, Earl," Goliath murmured, needing more. "Push them down."

Earl quickly obeyed, easing both his jeans and underwear halfway down his ass, freeing his erection. Immediately, Earl wrapped his long fingers around his thick shaft and jacked him. Groaning, he arched in Earl's hold, his balls quickly beginning to tingle.

"Earl," Goliath whined. "Oh, god."

Needing to do a little touching of his own, Goliath reached between them. He quickly gripped the waistband of his shifter's sweats. Pushing them down, he revealed the other man's hard cock. The engorged red shaft bobbed from a neatly trimmed bush of dark-blond curls, a bead of pre-cum pooling at the slit.

Even as Goliath's mouth watered with his desire to taste, he knew he wouldn't be able to wait. With his balls already tight and his shaft throbbing from the massage of Earl's lightly calloused hands, his body threatened to blow at any second. Needing his lover with him, Goliath gripped Earl's wrist and tugged the man's hand away from him.

Earl made a whine of distress, spurring Goliath to move quickly.

Goliath lowered his hips, pressing his leaking erection against the other man's. That earned him a whimpering moan from Earl. Needing to taste that, Goliath moved his head and pressed a hard kiss to Earl's lips.

As Earl opened to him, Goliath gripped both their dicks in his large hand. He tilted his hips, pushing harder against Earl's groin, applying more pressure. As Goliath began rocking, pushing his heavy balls against Earl's, he started a steady jacking.

Feeling Earl's nails dig into his upper arms while rocking into his ministrations, Goliath fed his man a grunt. He threaded the fingers of his other hand into Earl's thick hair, resting his weight on that forearm. His body vibrated as he ate at Earl's mouth, and he gave himself over to the pleasure of coupling with the man beneath him.

Just as Goliath felt certain he couldn't hold off his release,

Earl turned his head, breaking the kiss. His lover barked his name roughly, jolting beneath him. Earl's cock twitched in Goliath's hold as hot seed warmed his belly and chest.

The sting of Earl's nails in his arms, the feel of his body bowing beneath him, gave him that final push, and it was all over.

Goliath's orgasm crashed over his system. His cock pulsed as he added to the mess between them. His balls sent zings of bliss cascading through him, matching the hard jolts rocking his body.

Gritting his teeth, Goliath growled Earl's name. He squeezed his eyes shut, trembling and jerking. He barely had enough wherewithal to ease his hand even as he continued to jack them through their release.

When Goliath finally stopped coming, he eased his hand's movement. As he unwrapped his fingers, his shaft gave one more half-hearted spurt. He pressed his temple to Earl's and hummed as he floated on the endorphins of the best damn release he could ever remember.

*God. And from a hand job.*

"Oh, Earl," Goliath whispered, slowly coming back to himself. He felt his lover sliding his hands over his back and smiled. "So good." Turning his head a smidge, Goliath pressed a kiss to Earl's flesh before licking, tasting the man's delicious sweat. "Mmmm." A low chuckle escaped him. "You broke me."

Earl snicker-snorted, the noise making Goliath grin broadly.

"Well, I'm melted," Earl mumbled on a long sigh. "Your hand. Magick."

Gathering a bit of strength in his limbs, Goliath pushed up so he could look into Earl's eyes. He smiled upon spotting the man's heavy-lidded look. His relaxed, satisfied smile caused a warmth to unfurl in his gut.

*I put that look on this handsome man's face.*

Goliath began lifting his hand to Earl's face, intending to push the man's damp blond hair from his face. Noticing the cum on his fingers, he hesitated. Then, unable to resist, Goliath brought his hand to his lips. Licking over his fingers, he groaned softly as the salty, tangy fluid burst across his taste buds.

"We taste good," Goliath mumbled, meeting Earl's gaze. Seeing a flair of heat light up his brown eyes, as well as the way his lover eyed his hand, he smiled and eased it closer to the other man's mouth. "Wanna try?"

Earl gripped Goliath's wrist in a light hold.

At first, Goliath thought Earl would push his hand away. Instead, Earl drew it closer. He opened his mouth and stuck out his tongue. Sliding his appendage along a finger, Earl scooped up a large dollop.

Humming, Earl smiled as he met Goliath's gaze and swallowed. "You're so right. Delicious."

With a grin, Goliath swiped up some more cum before offering his hand once more. Over the next few minutes, they cleaned his hand together. Once it gleamed with their spit, Goliath clenched his fist and placed his forearm on the cushion beside Earl's head. Lowering his head, he captured his lover's mouth, enjoying the flavor of man and cum as he swept his tongue inside once more.

Goliath enjoyed a slow make-out session with Earl, their tongues tangling in a sensual dance. Every few minutes, they would break to breathe. Then he would capture Earl's mouth once more.

When Goliath's cock again threatened to harden, he lifted his head and smiled down at Earl.

"Your lips are addictive," Goliath rumbled before licking along Earl's bottom one. He barely resisted diving in once more, and that was only due to the itch starting at his groin.

With a sigh, Goliath began to ease away. "We should probably clean up, or we're gonna end up stuck together."

Earl winked. "I can think of worse things."

Goliath chuckled huskily. "Me, too."

Still, Goliath eased from between Earl's legs. A glance at the clock told him he was nearly out of time, too. He glanced at his chest and groin, seeing the white flakes caking his skin. Goliath saw that Earl was just as messy, and he found his attention snagged by the man's half-hard prick, which was splashed with globs of white. For a reason he decided not to analyze too closely, Goliath felt a wealth of smug satisfaction at marking his new lover.

Holding out his hand, Goliath wiggled his fingers. "Can I help you up?"

Earl groaned good-naturedly as he took Goliath's hand. Helping his lover to his feet, he took a step backward. Goliath held his jeans up with his spit-cleaned hand as he bent and pecked a kiss on Earl's lips once more.

What Goliath had told Earl was true. For some reason, he couldn't seem to get enough of the man's lips. They were smooth, soft, and warm. Combined with Earl's taste, Goliath feared he would have a hard time resisting him, even in public.

*That's certainly never happened before.*

Fortunately, Earl didn't seem to have a problem with it. His lover easily tipped his head back, accepting Goliath's attention. He welcomed it even, returning his kiss with enthusiasm.

Lifting his head, Goliath skimmed the backs of his clean hand along Earl's chin. Then he pushed his lover's hair back from his face. He really didn't want to leave, but a glance at the clock told him he needed to get a move on.

Acting on impulse, Goliath asked, "Wanna meet me at *Spiron's* tonight?"

Earl grinned, clearly pleased by the offer. "Yeah. I'd love

to."

"Great." Goliath pecked one last kiss to Earl's lips, then headed toward the kitchen, shuffling a little awkwardly. "Uh, I'll be there at six," he reminded him as he grabbed a paper towel and ran it under water in the sink. "Heard they had good pub food. Wings and shit."

Following him, Earl nodded. "Here. Let me get you a real cloth."

"You don't have to," Goliath countered, starting to wipe himself down with the damp paper towel. "This is fine."

Shoving his sweats down and off, Earl shook his head. "I'd like to."

Goliath found his gaze riveted to Earl's nude body as the man moved around the kitchen, comfortable and confident in his nakedness. He opened his mouth to tease him, then closed it just as quickly. Memories of that afternoon filled him, and he swallowed as thoughts of the paranormal flooded back.

*Right. He's a guy who can turn into a wolf. No wonder he's comfortable being naked.*

Rubbing the back of his neck with his free hand, Goliath knew he would need to process everything. Except, as Earl turned to him and began sliding a damp dish towel over his chest and groin, a fresh wave of arousal started heating him from the inside out. His prick began to thicken anew, and his skin goose bumped.

Goliath couldn't remember the last time a lover had taken the time to clean him.

*Does it really matter that Earl can turn into a wolf?*

# CHAPTER EIGHT

Earl stepped into *Spiron's Bar and Grill* and swept his gaze over the local watering hole. To the right were a number of tables and booths, only about half of them full. The bar area wrapped around to the left, separating the restaurant seating from the area boasting a number of pool tables, a dart board, and several small square tables lining the far wall. A number of guys already moved around the area—two playing pool with a few more calling out encouragement or pointers, as well as a couple of more playing darts.

Spotting Russell Vintners behind the bar, the wolf shifter owned the place, Earl tipped his chin up in greeting. The older wolf nodded back before heading toward a waiting customer. Russell had owned the bar for a couple of decades, and Earl had heard through the grapevine that the shifter was nearing that age where he needed to pull back from society and re-make his identity.

When Earl didn't spot Goliath, he headed to the bar. Using a foot, he snagged the leg of a stool and dragged it close. He positioned it so he could watch the door.

After serving the other customer, Russell headed his way. "Evenin,' Earl," he greeted. Leaning close, he sniffed discreetly. A smirk curved his lips as he asked, "What can I getcha?"

Earl refused to blush as he answered, "*Sam Adams* on tap."

Russell nodded and turned to fulfill the order.

After Goliath had left, Earl had refused to shower. He'd wanted to keep his mate's scent on him for as long as possible.

To that end, he'd wiped down in the bathroom, but he knew a paranormal's sensitive nose would pick up on the fact that he'd been intimate with someone recently.

When Russell returned, placing his beer before him, the older wolf arched one brow. "You don't normally advertise trysts quite like this, Earl," he stated in a low voice. "Why now?"

Unable to help himself, Earl grinned broadly. He rested his forearms on the bar, cradling the beer between them. "Met my mate," he murmured after a quick glance around. "New guy in town. Goliath Dickman."

Russell's eyes twitched just a little, probably in response to the name, before he smiled. "Good for you, Earl." Reaching across the bar, he patted his wrist. "I'm real happy for ya."

Earl grinned broadly. "Thanks." With a sigh, he thought about his man. "Didn't think it would happen so early in life, but gods, he's amazing."

Chuckling, Russell grabbed a cloth and began wiping the bar. "Yep. I know that feeling well."

The bar owner had his own fated mate. A lovely human woman named Seline. They'd been together for more years than Earl had been alive.

"You gonna have kids?" Russell asked.

Snorting, Earl rolled his eyes. "We met yesterday. I gotta claim him first." With a smirk, he added, "Plus, I'd like a few years alone with him before tossing kids into the mix." While Earl would eventually love a cute rugrat around, he mused, "Don't even know if Goliath wants kids."

Russell patted his wrist again. "Ya got plenty of time."

Earl nodded again, silently agreeing.

The door opened, and Nathan walked in. The deputy glanced around. Seeing as Goliath hadn't arrived and Earl knew his mate was supposed to buy him a drink, he lifted his hand and beckoned to the off-duty deputy.

While Earl didn't really know Nathan well—he'd served him at *Caribou's* a number of times and greeted him in passing on the street—he wondered if that would change. If he was going to be Goliath's friend, he wanted to get to know the human.

Even though Nathan appeared surprised, he still made his way over.

"Evening, Earl," Nathan greeted with a nod.

"Evening, Nathan," Earl replied. He indicated the stool to his left. "I know you're meeting Goliath here tonight. Hope you don't mind me joining you, too."

Nathan shrugged. "Not at all. And he said to call him Ollie." Then he turned to Russell. "Evening, Russell. Can I get a *Bud*?"

"Yep." Russell turned away to pour the drink.

Earl took that opportunity to share, "Actually, Goliath felt bad about not using the name his momma gave him, so I think he's going to return to his birth name." He shrugged upon seeing Nathan's surprised expression. Shrugging again, Earl added, "That's what he told me this afternoon, anyway."

"Saw him this afternoon, and now you're spending Saturday night with him?"

Taking in Nathan's arched brow and interested expression, Earl grinned broadly. "Yep. Met him last night at *Caribou's*, and well . . . when you hit on something amazing, ya gotta grab on with both hands fast." When he saw Nathan smirk, he added, "Besides. You've seen the man. He's fucking hot. Can't let him get snatched up by someone else."

While Earl said the words in jest, just the idea of Goliath with anyone else made him want to growl.

"Not my type, but good for you," Nathan told him as Russell arrived with his beer. "Thanks, Russ."

"You're welcome," the shifter replied. "You boys need anything else?"

Earl nodded. "Can I get two orders of hot wings?" Then, recalling Goliath's meal the prior evening, he added, "And two sets of potato skins?"

Russ nodded. "Sure thing." He turned to Nathan. "And you?"

Nathan hummed as he swallowed the sip of beer he'd taken. "A personal pepperoni and sausage pizza with mushrooms and black olives."

Grinning, Russ nodded. "Sounds good." Then Russ turned and headed to the computer to input the order.

Earl knew that Russ's system was similar to *Caribou's*. Both places were shifter owned, so when the pack had updated *Caribou's*, they'd updated *Spiron's*, too. Russ didn't even need to leave the bar. He would input the request into the terminal, and it would appear on a screen in the back.

*Gotta love technology.*

While Earl knew that Russell had bitched about the new-fangled technology for at least a year, he'd quieted down since then.

Noticing the door open again, Earl grinned when he saw Goliath. His mate had to duck his head and turn his body to enter. He even glanced up, as if checking the height of the ceiling, before surveying the space.

When Goliath spotted Earl, he smiled and started toward him. "Hey, Earl," he greeted. After a second of hesitation and a quick glance around, he dipped his head and pressed a kiss to Earl's cheek, sending a wealth of pleasure through him. Butterflies even bumped in his belly. Goliath cleared his throat as he straightened, a shy smile curving his lips as he took the stool to Earl's right. "Uh, evening, Nathan. Sorry I'm late." Goliath pointed at his beer. "I'll get your next one. Yeah?"

Nathan bobbed his head in a nod. "Sure, but you really didn't have to, man." He leaned on the bar, giving Earl's mate a smile. "We're good."

Even as Goliath nodded, he stated, "Yeah, but it'll make me feel better."

After another nod, Nathan grinned and asked, "So you and Earl, eh?"

"Yep," Goliath replied without hesitation, pleasing Earl to no end.

"Good for you," Nathan responded. After taking a sip of beer, he asked, "How long did you work in Nashville?"

"Twelve years," Goliath replied. "Went to the academy there."

Nathan nodded. "Well, we're happy to have you out here. We needed more good men."

"Thanks." Goliath smiled as he glanced Earl's way. "I'm pleased to be here."

Russell arrived and held his hand out over the bar. "I'm Russell Vintners. Bar owner. You're the new deputy, right?"

Goliath dipped his chin in a swift nod before taking Russell's hand. "Yes, sir. Goliath Dickman. Good to meet you."

"You, too, Goliath." Russell peered up at him. "Your mother must have been clairvoyant to name you so well." Resting his hand on the bar, he asked, "What can I get ya, son?"

Earl noticed a slight pinkish hue tinging Goliath's cheeks as his mate answered, "Uh . . ." He peered beyond Russell at the taps on the wall. "How about an *Amberbock*."

"You got it." Russell moved away.

Touching Goliath's hand where it rested on the bar, Earl asked, "You okay?" He knew his mate was a little sensitive about his name.

Goliath sighed. "You'd think I'd be used to it by now," he murmured softly, glancing Russell's way before meeting Earl's gaze. "I'm good."

"You know he meant your height and size," Earl replied quietly, although considering Russell was a shifter, he knew the man would be able to hear every word they spoke if he wanted to. With a wink, Earl leaned close and hissed, "Not everything is about—" He glanced down at Goliath's crotch and waggled his eyebrows. "Even though it's a thing of beauty."

Snorting, Goliath rolled his eyes. He grinned and chuckled softly. Leaning over, he bumped his shoulder into Earl's.

Pleased to have relaxed his mate, Earl straightened on his stool. "I ordered wings and skins. Hope you're hungry."

As if on cue, Goliath's stomach grumbled.

Earl chuckled.

"Guess I am," Goliath rumbled, his dark eyes twinkling. Leaning on the bar, he asked, "You grow up around here, Nathan?"

"Yep," Nathan replied. "Born and raised." He smiled as he revealed, "Wouldn't want to live anywhere else."

Sipping his beer, Earl relaxed on his stool. He listened to Goliath and Nathan get to know each other, learning more about both humans. Earl found himself surprised to find out Nathan loved hiking and riding a motorcycle, and he realized he actually had quite a bit in common with the human.

*Huh. Gonna have to invite him to our next poker night.*

Nathan offered to show Goliath a few good hiking trails when they both shared a day off, including Earl in the offer. After agreeing to check their schedules, they decided to plan something. Their food arrived and the conversation slowed as they ate, ordering another round of beers.

As promised, Goliath asked Russell to put Nathan's beer on his tab.

As Russell placed their beers before them, he leaned toward them on the bar. "You stayin' for the band?"

"Band?" Earl arched a brow.

Russell pointed toward the pool area. In the corner, a group of three men were setting up instruments. "New thing," he told them. "Live music one Saturday a month." Russell shrugged. "For now. We'll see how it goes."

"Huh." Nathan picked up a piece of pizza. Before taking a bite, he asked, "How long have you been doing that?"

Earl wondered the same thing.

"First time," Russell revealed. As feedback echoed through a speaker, the wolf shifter winced. "Not sure I'm gonna like it, but since I'm thinkin' about sellin,' we'll see."

Having cringed right along with the older wolf, Earl nodded absently.

"What?" Nathan frowned. "You can't sell, Russell. You're a feature here. Been running this place ever since I can remember." He waved his hand to indicate Russell. "And you look great. Surely you have plenty more years."

Russell chuckled as he smirked at Nathan. "I'm older than I look, son." Seeing someone wave from the other end of the bar, he dipped his chin in a nod and headed that way.

"Well, damn," Nathan muttered, shaking his head. "Never thought I'd see the day Russ didn't own this place."

Earl clicked his tongue as he nodded. "It'll be a change, that's for sure." Trying to sound encouraging, he added, "Maybe he'll change his mind and stick around for a few more years."

Except, he really didn't think so.

Another squeal of feedback erupted through the room for a heartbeat. Wincing, Earl glanced around. He noticed a number of other shifters in the room, and he wasn't the only one affected by the obnoxious noise.

"Well, if it's the first band, I think I better stay," Nathan commented absently. He lifted his beer and glanced between Earl and Goliath. "It'll be interesting to see if the crowd gets a little rowdy."

Goliath nodded slowly, his eyebrows furrowing. "Yeah. We might just need to be here to keep the peace."

Nathan tipped his mug in salute before taking a sip.

While Earl had zero desire to sit through a band, he nodded anyway. Another thought hit, and he smirked at his lover. "Maybe they'll play something we can dance to."

Goliath's eyes widened. He swallowed hard enough to cause his Adam's apple to bob. Then he took a swig of beer.

Earl scented Goliath's nerves, so he reached over and patted his hand. "We don't have to, Goliath," he assured with a smile. "It was just a random thought."

With a deep sigh, Goliath asked, "Would the people here really not care if two guys danced together?"

Nathan grinned at him. "There are so many gay couples around here, that if someone did say something derogatory, they'd probably end up decked." He pointed to a booth to the right. "That's Kade McGraw. He owns a mechanic shop. He's sitting with his husband, Tom. Across from them are Manon Lemelle and his husband, Chris." Twirling his finger to indicate the room, Nathan told him, "And I could name a few more gay couples interspersed around the room."

"Damn." Goliath peered around the bar, obviously surprised. "Really?"

"Yep." Nathan pointed to a table. "That's Rainy MacDougal and his husband, Travis, sitting with Cliff MacDougal and his wife, Lisa. Rainy and Cliff are brothers, and Travis and Lisa are brother and sister." With a snort, he added, "Raised a few eyebrows when that pair married into the same family."

"Rainy." Goliath halted on that name and turned to Earl. "Didn't you have a Rainy out running with you in, uh" — he hesitated, glancing from Nathan to Rainy and back to Earl — "in the woods this afternoon?"

Earl nodded, appreciating that Goliath had caught himself. "Yes, I did go running with Rainy today." He suddenly rose. "I'm going to go ask Travis how Nedrick is doing."

"Something happen to Ned?" Nathan asked.

Grimacing, Earl racked his brain for something plausible,

"He was out with me and Rainy." He shook his head as he came up with, "Ended up popping his ankle pretty good on some rough terrain. Cliff and Rainy took him to the doc."

Nathan nodded. "Bummer. Hope he's doing okay."

"Me, too." After squeezing Goliath's upper arm, Earl assured, "Be right back."

Goliath nodded.

As Earl moved across the bar, he felt the hairs on his nape stand on end. A glance over his shoulder showed him that Goliath was tracking his movements. Smiling to himself, he returned his attention to where he was going.

"Hey, guys," Earl greeted as he stopped at the tall table where the foursome were sitting. "Here for the band?"

Lisa nodded, smiling. "I haven't heard a band in years, so we got a sitter." She turned to Cliff, whose hand she held. "The guys are kind enough to sit through it with us."

Earl exchanged a commiserating look with Cliff and Rainy. Sometimes, having shifter senses made certain things tough. Being dragged to a live show was one of those times.

There was probably a reason Russell hadn't bothered with a band before, as at least half of his patrons were fellow shifters.

Turning to Rainy, Earl asked, "How are you feeling?"

Rainy grimaced. "Probably better than you." Keeping his voice low, he leaned close and whispered, "I heard you got stuck with that damn serum. How's your wolf?"

Earl grimaced, tipping his head to the side a little. "Can't feel 'em much, but every once in a while I get a sense of him. I'll be okay." Not really wanting to discuss how unsettled he felt about missing his other half, Earl asked Travis, "And Nedrick?"

"Bullet lodged in his haunch," Travis told him, keeping his voice low. "Lark removed it and stitched him up. Since I'm a vet, he asked me to double-check his work." Scoffing softly, he murmured, "He's getting damn good at working on animals, but I know he's still a little uncomfortable with it." Smiling tightly, Travis added, "Nedrick will make a full recovery. It'll just take a few weeks."

"Good," Earl whispered. Shaking his head, he frowned. "Still can't believe we all missed their scents."

Growling softly, Cliff grumbled, "With hunters in the area, we all need to up our vigilance."

"You can say that again," Earl agreed. Hearing the band start, he turned to head back to his own date.

"Hey, Earl," Cliff interrupted with a smile and a teasing sniff. "Congratulations."

Earl grinned. "Thanks."

# CHAPTER NINE

Goliath glanced to his right once more, unable to help keeping an eye on Earl. There was just something about the handsome man that drew his attention like a moth to a flame. He filled out his jeans to perfection, and Goliath constantly had to resist easing his fingers through his hair to tuck the blond locks behind his ear.

"Got it bad already, huh?"

Returning his focus to Nathan, Goliath smiled ruefully. "Chemistry like that can hit fast." Even before hearing about all the shifter mating bullshit, he'd been drawn to him.

*And now that I've touched him, kissed him, I want him even more.*

Nathan nodded slowly, a smile curving his lips. "It really does . . . or so I've seen." His expression turned wry. "Never felt that connection myself."

"I've never felt anything this intense, either," Goliath admitted. "I—"

The band started playing, and Nathan cocked his head as if trying to listen better. Goliath realized the loud music was making it difficult to hold a conversation. He eased onto the stool Earl had been using, drawing closer to Nathan so he could try again.

"I've never felt anything this intense, either," Goliath repeated, and Nathan nodded in understanding. With a shrug, he added, "If it burns out just as fast, then so be it, but I'm willing to give it a shot."

Considering Earl and Declan had been talking about mates—soul mates and bonding and shit, not that he had all the particulars—Goliath had a funny suspicion that Earl didn't plan to let him go anytime soon.

*And I'm okay with that.*

Smiling, Nathan nodded. "Yep. Totally smitten." Then he sobered as he knocked his shoulder into Goliath's upper arm. "I'm a little jealous, actually." Rubbing his hand over his mouth, Nathan frowned into his beer. "Been watching a lot of guys find that special someone over the last decade or so. Still waiting for it to happen to me."

Goliath felt sympathy for his new friend. Patting his upper arm, he told him, "I'm sure it'll hit you before too long." He snorted, adding, "And when you least expect it, too." With a roll of his eyes, Goliath smirked at Nathan. "That seems to be how it works."

Nathan smiled and nodded at him. Then he sobered as he looked at someone behind Goliath.

Feeling a hand on his arm, Goliath turned, expecting it to be Earl. Instead, he found a blonde woman who looked vaguely familiar standing beside his stool. As much as Goliath wanted to pull his arm away from her touch, his momma had taught him to always be polite to women. Plus, Goliath was a deputy, a servant of the people.

"Evening," Goliath greeted, trying to keep the wariness out of his tone. "Can I help you, ma'am?"

The appreciative gleam in her blue eyes as she swept her gaze up and down him sort of made him feel like a piece of meat. While he liked that look from Earl, he didn't appreciate it from this woman. He wasn't certain why, but it was the truth.

She giggled—actually *giggled*—while smiling coyly at him through her lashes. "Oh, wow. So sweet," she crooned. After biting her lip provocatively, she continued, "But no need to call me ma'am. I'm Emily, and you can help me by asking me to dance."

*Dance?*

Goliath flicked his gaze toward where the band played. Sure enough, there were already couples filling the space where people stood to throw darts, using it as a make-shift dance floor. There were also people dancing in between the pool table and the square tables.

*Damn. That's a fire hazard waiting to happen.*

Returning his attention to Emily, Goliath racked his brain for a polite way to get out of dancing with her. He didn't want to hurt her feelings, but he didn't want to hold her either. If he were to dance with anyone, it would be Earl.

"I, uh . . ." Goliath started slowly.

Goliath glanced toward Nathan, but he was eating his last piece of pizza. He also sported just a hint of a smile as he studiously focused on his food.

*No help there. Jerk.*

"I'm flattered, Emily," Goliath began again. Spotting Earl heading his way, he felt a swell of relief. The annoyed narrowing of Earl's eyes was even sort of hot. "But I'm here with someone."

Emily glanced toward Nathan, perhaps misunderstanding. "Oh, Deputy Nathan won't mind if I steal you. Will you, Deputy?"

After swallowing a bite of food, Nathan peered at the woman. "Just Nathan right now, Emily." He smiled as he tipped his hat. "I'm off duty."

Goliath smirked as he eyed the other deputy. "A deputy is never off duty," he teased.

Letting out a soft scoff, Nathan nodded in acknowledgment. "But I *am* out of uniform," he countered.

"And I didn't mean Nathan," Goliath told Emily. Resting his hand over the woman's, he gripped it gently and tugged it from his arm. He used his chin to jerk in the direction of his approaching lover. "I mean I'm here with Earl."

"Earl?" Emily repeated incredulously. There was even a hint of distaste in her tone. After a glance in Earl's direction, she returned her attention to Goliath. "Oh, Deputy," Emily crooned, revealing she'd known exactly who he was before she'd approached. Pressing closer, she pushed her breasts against his arm. Emily also continued to squeeze Goliath's fingers when he tried to release her. "You're new in town, so believe me when I tell you that you don't want to get mixed up with those sorts of people." Standing on her toes, Emily tried to get even closer, pursing her lips as if to kiss him. "If you do, even if you're bisexual, you'll be labeled a fag."

Goliath just managed to keep down his snarl, and he noticed Nathan stiffening beside him. Leaning back on his stool, he used his free hand to grip her shoulder. He pushed her back a pace.

"Those aren't very nice words coming from your lips," Goliath stated with a shake of his head. "Please let go of my hand now, ma'am."

Short of waving his hand as if shaking off a bug, Goliath wasn't certain how to get rid of Emily's unwanted touch.

"Emily," Earl stated by way of greeting, stopping beside him.

Emily's blue eyes narrowed just a little as she glanced Earl's way, but she didn't bother to respond. Instead, she turned back to Goliath. Emily smiled again. Her eyes narrowed as she placed her free hand on top of Goliath's where it still rested on her shoulder, making certain she didn't move closer. Suddenly, he felt her attempt to slide his hand downward, as if she wanted him to touch her lower . . . like he was going to feel up her tits.

Goliath yanked away his hand as if scalded.

*What the hell?*

"Come on, Deputy Goliath," Emily purred, immediately moving back into his space. "Let's go dance. I wanna feel your big hands on me."

"Emily, back off," Earl growled. His hands flexed as if he were fighting his desire to yank her away from Goliath. "He already told you no."

Goliath wasn't certain how Earl knew that, but he seconded his assertion. "I told you I'm here with Earl, Emily." He again tried to drop her hand, but he was a little too worried to grip her shoulder and push her away again. "Please find someone else to dance with."

As Emily's eyes narrowed, lighting with a calculated gleam, Goliath suddenly recalled where he'd seen her before. She was the waitress who'd interrupted him and Earl the prior evening at *Caribou's*. Goliath had noticed her veiled hostile glances at Earl. He wondered if the woman's advances on him were just a ruse to needle his lover.

Either way, Goliath wasn't going to let it work.

"I want to dance with you, Deputy," Emily insisted, placing her free hand on his thigh and squeezing. "I know if you give me a chance, I can convince you we'll be great together."

As Emily spoke, she began sliding her hand higher up his thigh.

"Back off, Emily." Earl gripped Emily's upper arm and pulled, effectively yanking her away from Goliath. "He said no," he snarled. "No means no."

Emily cried out and flinched as if in pain. Twisting away from Earl, she brought her left hand to her right upper arm. She gripped it while letting out a sob, tears forming in her eyes.

"Earl assaulted me, Deputy Nathan," Emily claimed, her voice full of pain and anger. "You saw." She blinked furiously as if trying to fight back tears. "I want him arrested!"

Deputy Nathan scowled at the woman, turning to face her on his stool. "Emily, we both know he didn't assault you." Crossing his arms over his chest, he shook his head. "What the hell are you trying to do?"

"He did, too," Emily countered, pushing out her bottom lip. "Earl put his hands on me and jerked me." She lifted her hand and looked at her arm. "I bet I'll end up with bruises."

There was nothing there.

A pair of women moved to flank Emily. "We saw the whole thing," the brunette declared. She scowled at Earl with narrowed eyes. "Earl grabbed Emily and yanked her."

"Yeah," another woman with brown hair began. She pointed at Emily. "Look at how Emily is holding her arm. Earl hurt her."

Earl rolled his eyes as he sidled closer to Goliath, putting himself between them. "You're being a little dramatic, Emily." Stepping back a bit, he pressed his hip into Goliath's thigh. "You just want me gone so you can keep trying to hit on my man."

Emily opened her mouth again, but Nathan cut in. "Emily, if you expect me to take Earl in for pulling you away from Deputy Goliath, then I'll have to take you in for putting your hands all over Deputy Goliath when he told you no." Frowning at the woman, he asked, "Is that what you want?"

With her cheeks taking on a pinkish hue, Emily frowned at Nathan. "That's absolutely preposterous. I'm going to report you to the sheriff for not doing your job," she claimed. "You—"

"Are making a spectacle in my bar, ma'am," Russell cut in. At some point, he'd rounded said bar, and he currently stood near the vacated stool. "I'm going to have to ask you three ladies to either leave these gentlemen alone or leave my bar."

Emily gasped, looking completely outraged, not to mention shocked. "What?" she gasped. With wide eyes, she glanced around the room. "But—" Emily paused.

Goliath took a quick glance around, too. He realized they were the center of attention for just about everyone nearby. The only ones not paying attention was the band as well as those dancing.

Even as Goliath fought back a grimace — he hated being the center of attention unless it was in the line of duty — he realized most of the people were eyeing Emily with scowls, distaste, or as if she had two heads.

Emily obviously didn't have the support of the room, and she must have realized it. "Typical that you'd take their side," she huffed, resting one hand on her hip. Pointing at Nathan, Emily declared, "And don't think for a moment that I won't report you."

Spinning dramatically, Emily flounced from the bar, followed by her two friends. One of which paused at the door. She hurried toward their booth and grabbed a pair of purses, then rushed to catch up with her friends.

"What a bunch of drama llamas," Earl grumbled, shaking his head even as he continued to press into Goliath's side. He rested his hand on Goliath's knee and peered up at him. "You okay?"

Sighing deeply, Goliath shrugged. "Not sure what that was all about, to be honest." He scowled as he glanced from the bartender, who had moved back behind the bar, to Nathan and Earl. "Is she always like that?"

Earl grimaced, making no move to ease away from Goliath. "Not sure. She started working at *Caribou's* a month ago," he told him. "Before that, I hadn't really associated with her or her clique."

"Well, she seems to have it out for you, Earl," Russell stated, looking over his shoulder at them as he poured a beer. "Keep your eyes open." He arched a brow and met Goliath's gaze. "You, too, Deputy. Emily doesn't seem to like being told no."

"Yes, sir," Goliath replied absently, silently agreeing with the bar's owner.

Earl squeezed his knee, gaining his attention. "You okay,

Goliath?" Concern filled his pretty brown eyes. "We can leave, too, if you'd like."

*Do I want to leave?*

Goliath glanced around again. Most everyone had gone back to their own business. A few people glanced furtively at him before their attention strayed elsewhere. Goliath glanced toward the dancers again and noticed a couple of men two-stepping together.

The music changed to something slower.

Returning his focus to Earl, Goliath murmured, "I recall you saying you wanted to dance." He gripped Earl's hand, lifting it from his knee. "Let's do that before we go."

As Goliath led Earl to an available space near the pool table and wrapped him in his arms, he took in Earl's smile. He swayed to the music, holding the shorter man close. That look, and feeling his lover's body against his own, made all the stares worth it.

# CHAPTER TEN

"Earl."

Turning from where he hung his jacket on a hook in the employee lounge, Earl gave his attention to Kolton Bindres. The human was the manager on shift that evening at *Caribou's*. He stood just inside the door with a serious expression on his tanned features.

"Yes, Mister Bindres?" Earl asked, a slither of unease trickling up his spine upon taking in the man's tense stance.

"I need to see you in the office before you start your shift."

"Of course, sir," Earl replied, forcing a smile he didn't feel.

Kolton turned and headed out of the room. He turned left toward the office and store rooms. A right would have taken him past the restrooms, one of the doors to the kitchen, and finally to the restaurant proper.

After putting his phone on silent, Earl shoved it into his back pocket and sighed. He followed after the human. Earl reached the office door, gave the mostly closed piece of wood a perfunctory knock, then headed inside.

Kolton already sat behind the desk. "Please, close the door and have a seat." He indicated the chair before the desk.

Earl obeyed, appreciating his phone's protective cover so he didn't crush it. Resting his hands on his thighs, he held Kolton's gaze and waited.

After a sigh, Kolton leaned forward, resting his elbows on the desk. He steepled his fingers before him. Eyeing him, Kolton tapped his forefingers against his lips for a moment, perhaps gathering his thoughts.

Finally, Kolton lowered his hands and folded them before him. "There's no easy way to say this," he finally began. "I've received a couple of complaints about you."

"Complaints?" Earl couldn't keep the confusion out of his voice. "About my service?"

Kolton lifted his hands in a *sort of* gesture. "A couple of customers have commented how you're too busy flirting with certain types of customers to keep up with your duties."

Earl felt a flush threaten to darken his neck, and he fought to control it. He wasn't entirely certain if it was from embarrassment or anger. Earl definitely felt a certain level of frustration.

"Flirting?" Earl repeated slowly.

Kolton nodded.

He cleared his throat as he recalled meeting Goliath on Friday evening. That had been the only time he'd ever flirted with a customer. Just that fast, he knew who was behind the complaints.

*Emily. Damn it.*

"Now, I understand wanting to get good tips," Kolton continued slowly, obviously choosing his words carefully. "But you need to be careful. There's a line you can't cross." Tapping the desk restlessly, he added, "And you certainly can't spend extra time with certain types of customers at the detriment of our other guests."

Cocking his head, Earl asked, "Did these complaints offer something specific?" When Kolton's eyes narrowed, he quickly added, "Examples of what I did." Earl pasted on a pained smile. "I try to treat all my guests equally unless they force me not to," he continued, rubbing his thumb over the seam of his jeans. "I need to know what upset someone."

"Someone reported you leaning over the bar and whispering to a male customer," Kolton told him, his cheeks taking on just a hint of pink. "You allowed the customer to touch your hand and jaw." Grimacing, he quickly added, "If this was a night club or bar, you could get away with that. But not here."

Before Earl could comment, Kolton told him, "Another time you were leaning over a male customer and pointing at the menu, but I guess they seemed to think you were doing it as a come-on." Sighing, he scrubbed his palm over his face as he sat back in his chair. "Perhaps you were leaning into the man. Again, I think it has to do with the touching aspect."

"I'll be careful to keep a respectful distance between myself and customers," Earl began, trying to reassure the manager. Then he cocked his head and frowned. "Although, those instances were just Friday night, and the guy at the bar was a friend, and the guy at the table was my boyfriend."

While, technically, Earl and Goliath hadn't been boyfriends at the time, they damn sure were now. They'd spent the prior evening making out, exploring each other, and talking more about shifters. Earl had enjoyed cuddling on the sofa before the fire, taking the opportunity to reiterate some of what he and Alpha Declan had already shared about mates and bonding. He'd also explained how it was done and what it would mean for their relationship—generally, that it was marriage with no chance of divorce.

Earl had also explained the perks that came with it. He'd shared how Goliath would take on some of the attributes of shifters, like increased strength, speed, and health. Earl had also explained that he would never stray and he would devote his life to his mate's happiness, pleasure, and health.

Goliath had ended up a little overwhelmed, and he was taking that evening to digest everything.

While Earl appreciated the fact that the serum had worn off and he could feel his wolf again, his animal was riding him hard to head straight to his mate's after work. Instead, Earl had promised to give his human time. They planned to meet up for brunch the next day before either of them had to work.

He knew it was going to be a long night.

This dressing down was just making it longer.

"Well, perhaps spending so much time with your friends meant you weren't as attentive to your other customers," Kolton mused, rubbing his chin. "Either way, I'm putting that I gave you a warning in your file. Please be careful in the future."

Earl nodded slowly, accepting that. "Yes, sir. I'll be mindful not to spend too much time with any specific customer, even friends or family."

Kolton stared at Earl for a moment, and Earl remained quiet. He didn't know what the human expected him to say. Earl wouldn't apologize for his behavior, since he knew it was all pretty benign.

"Okay." Kolton nodded. "Best get to work then."

Nodding again, Earl rose to his feet and headed out of the office. He grabbed a small order pad and pen, although he rarely ever needed it. Earl was pretty good at committing requests to memory unless a customer decided to make changes to something.

As Earl checked the seating chart to see where he was assigned, he noticed Emily heading toward the order kiosk. She glanced his way, offering him a cold smirk. Then she lifted her nose to the air with a sniff before focusing on entering her order.

Gritting his teeth, Earl dismissed her. He appreciated that he was working on the other side of the restaurant. As he got to work, another random thought entered his mind.

*I wonder what would have happened if she'd taken her complaints to Jacomo?*

Jacomo was another of *Caribou's* managers, and he was a fellow wolf shifter. He would have scented Emily's lies, seeing through her ruse.

*I wonder what would have happened then?*

After finishing his shift at seven that evening, Earl felt restless. He thought about going for a run, but recalling the hunters, he dismissed the idea. Instead, he decided to check on Nedrick.

Earl drove to Alpha Declan's house. Knocking on the front door, he waited on the front porch, shoving his hands into his pockets. When the door opened, Earl smiled at Lark.

"Hey, Earl," the alpha mate greeted, stepping back and swinging the door wide. "How are you doing." Waggling his brows, he teased, "How's the mate seduction going?"

"Good, I think," Earl replied, entering the large, lodge-style home. "He stayed the night, and we spent a lot of time talking."

Lark snickered, shutting the door behind him. "Talking, huh?" With a wink, he teased, "Is that what the kids are calling it these days?"

Snorting, Earl rolled his eyes. He refused to blush as he thought about the *other things* they'd done together. Earl pushed those thoughts aside, since all they would do was have his body popping wood.

"I thought I'd swing by and visit Ned," Earl told Lark. "Which room is he in upstairs?"

While half the bottom floor was dominated by an open-concept living, dining, and kitchen space, the other half contained the alpha's wing. He had a large study for meeting with pack members, as well as his and Lark's bedroom suite, and a library. The upstairs of the lodge had been remodeled years before. There were four bedrooms, two bathrooms, and two rooms set up as medical rooms. Earl knew Declan had set up the basement as a sort of lab for Lark, but he'd never been down there. Rumor had it there was a holding cell down there, too.

"I'm sure he'd like the company," Lark told him, leading the way toward the stairs beside the dining room. "He's in the first room on the left."

"Thanks." Earl started up the stairs.

"Tell him dinner will be ready in about twenty minutes," Lark told him. "You should join us, too."

Earl smiled at the kind, blond human. "Thanks. I'll let him know."

As if on cue, Earl's stomach rumbled, making Lark laugh.

With a grin, Earl took the stairs two at a time. He reached the second floor and headed to the indicated room. After knocking, he heard his friend call for him to enter.

Earl opened the door and slipped inside. "Hey, man," he greeted, moving forward. "How are ya?"

He smiled at Nedrick, finding the dirty-blond-haired wolf shifter lounging in bed. There was a bandage on his left hip, just noticeable over the waistband of his sweatpants. That leg was being propped up on pillows.

Ned grinned at him. "Hey, Earl." Scoffing, he glanced at his leg, then shrugged. "Could be worse." He sobered, turning serious. "A lot worse."

Nodding in agreement, Earl headed toward the chair in front of the desk. "You got that right." He dragged it toward the bed and settled backward on it, placing his arms along the back. "Gods, I can't believe we missed scenting those damn hunters."

Grimacing, Ned nodded.

"I was sorry to hear you'll have to do therapy, but Travis said you'll make a full recovery," Earl continued. Reaching out, he squeezed Ned's wrist. "If you need help with anything, please let me know."

"Thanks, man, but you should be focusing on your new mate, not me," Nedrick countered. With a waggle of his brows, he claimed, "I heard that he was the one who saved us. I hope you rewarded him . . . a lot."

Earl chuckled as he grinned at his friend. "Oh, definitely."

"So, tell me about him," Nedrick encouraged. With a twinkle in his brown eyes, he began, "I hear his name is Goliath Dickman. Does he live up to —"

"Hey," Earl snapped, pointing at his friend. "Don't you finish that."

Chuckling, Nedrick lifted his hands in placation. "Sorry. Couldn't resist."

Earl heaved a sigh as he rolled his eyes. "Of course, you couldn't." He let the ire roll off his back, but he remained serious as he stated, "Goliath is pretty sensitive about that, so please don't pull that shit when you meet him."

Nedrick nodded quickly. "Absolutely. I'll be good."

Then Earl sighed, and he would forever deny the way his voice came out sort of dreamy. "And he totally lives up to his name . . . in every way." He saw Nedrick's grin return as he continued, "Goliath is a six foot eight mountain of a man. He's totally proportional." Recalling the evening before, Earl added, "He has to turn his body and duck his head when going through a door. He can pick me up and carry me. His hands are the size of dinner plates, and the way he palms my ass . . ."

"Whoa, whoa. TMI, man," Nedrick interrupted with a laugh. A fond smile etched across his features, he told Earl, "I'm really happy for you." Then his brows furrowed. "But what the hell are you doing here with me?"

Earl grimaced as he rubbed the back of his neck. "I had to work this afternoon, and he asked for the evening to decompress," he admitted with a shrug. "We're meeting at *Mama's Diner* tomorrow at eleven for brunch. Then we both work in the afternoon."

Nedrick nodded slowly. "I hear that humans need a little time. How does he seem? Accepting?"

"He really does," Earl replied, recalling their time together. "With humans, they get tripped up with how quickly we need our mates with us, so he's struggling with that," he reminded his buddy. "Hell, he just moved here and is still acclimating, so this is a shock to the system on top of that change."

"Yeah." Nedrick nodded in commiseration.

"Oh, hey." Earl rose to his feet and began pushing the chair away. "Dinner is about ready." He moved closer to the bed. "Can I give you a hand heading down there?"

Nedrick nodded, grunting as he eased to a sitting position. "Sure."

Earl quickly slipped an arm under Nedrick's lower back, offering him support so he didn't have to put as much strain on his leg. In short order, he helped his buddy to his feet. Keeping his arm around the other shifter, Earl helped him limp out of the room and down the stairs.

In the dining room, Earl saw that Alpha Declan was busy setting the table. "Evening, Earl," his alpha greeted, smiling in welcome. He pointed a knife at a cushioned chair. "That's for Ned."

Once Earl had Nedrick positioned, he asked, "Can I help with anything?"

Declan glanced over his shoulder at Lark, who was scooping slices of fried potatoes onto a platter. "How about ye grab everyone drinks?" The alpha headed toward the sliding glass door leading to the deck. "I'll take a beer from the fridge."

Earl nodded. "Will do." Heading toward the fridge, he asked, "What would you like, Lark?"

"Glass of white wine for me, please." Lark used his spatula to indicate the wine rack built into the bottom of the cupboard to the left of the fridge. "The bottle to the very left, please."

Grabbing the indicated bottle, Earl saw it was a nice Riesling. "You mind if I have some?"

"Of course not," Lark replied as he headed to the table with the platter. "Help yourself."

That was one of the things Earl absolutely loved about Declan and his pack. His alpha and his mate were very laidback. They shared their good fortune with everyone in the pack and made certain everyone had everything they needed to be well taken care of.

After popping the cork, Earl placed the bottle on the counter. He pulled down two stemware from the rack under the bottles and placed them next to it. Earl poured some into each, then peered toward Nedrick.

"What about you, Ned?"

Ned relaxed in his chair and stared at the food hungrily. "I'll take a beer with the alpha."

Earl nodded and found an assortment of wine stoppers in the drawer under the rack. Choosing one, a metal rearing horse figurine, he pressed the cork into the top. Then he carried the bottle and filled glasses to the table. After that, he found the beers Declan had indicated.

Declan came in bearing a tray of sizzling steaks. Their aroma immediately filled the dining room, causing Earl's mouth to water. He hummed appreciatively as he eased into a seat.

After placing a small steak on Lark's plate and a much larger one on his own, Declan passed the platter to Earl. "So," his alpha started. "What's this I hear about ye having trouble at *Caribou's*?"

With a groan, Earl chose a steak for himself and Nedrick. He took a couple of scoops of the fried potato slices, followed by some green beans. Picking up his knife and fork, Earl cut into the juicy steak as he began explaining his trouble with Emily.

# CHAPTER ELEVEN

"Dad, how did you know Mom was the one?"

Goliath sat in his recliner, his feet kicked up, holding his second cup of coffee for the day. A glance at the clock told him he still had an hour before he needed to leave to meet Earl for brunch. He'd taken the prior evening to think and process, and now he was ready to reach out for advice.

"You meet someone, son?" Barton's excited voice came through the line. "You've only been there a couple of weeks. You move fast."

Scoffing, Goliath knew that his father had no idea. The prior morning, cuddling with Earl after a mutual tug-off session, the wolf shifter had explained how he wanted to bond with Goliath and have him move in with him as soon as possible. Having never been in a relationship, he hadn't been certain what to think of that.

"Yeah, I met someone," Goliath admitted, thinking of his lover. His voice grew soft. "A great guy named Earl Raukus. He's . . . special."

"I can't wait to meet him," his father replied. His voice grew quiet as he asked, "When you think about this Earl, how do you feel? What comes to mind?"

Goliath took a sip of coffee, rolling the question around in his mind. "Well." Setting the mug aside, he tipped his head back and relaxed on the cushion. "He has this smooth tenor voice that I could listen to all day," Goliath began, smiling at the ceiling. "His eyes are this warm dark chocolate color I could stare into all day. When he touches my hand, I get goose bumps."

He decided not to share how his dick went ramrod straight just in the man's presence . . . or just thinking about the man.

"We danced in the local bar last night, and his smile was the only thing I could see, even though I knew there were people staring." Goliath felt his blood heat upon recalling how good it'd felt to hold Earl while swaying to the music. "And his kiss. God."

His father's warm chuckle sounded through the line. "I think you just answered your own question, Goliath." The man sounded pleased. "You get that spare room set up? I wanna meet him."

"I was thinking about moving in with him." Goliath blurted that out before he could second guess himself.

"Oh." Barton fell silent for several seconds before clearing his throat. "When did you meet Earl again?"

Goliath knew he hadn't actually told his father that, yet. "Uh, Friday night," he admitted. Before his father could say more, he answered his original question. "Yes. I have the spare bedroom set up."

"If you don't mind my asking, why are you in such a gol-darn hurry?"

Due to the fact that Goliath couldn't explain about shifters and bonding, he took a moment to formulate a good answer. He really couldn't. "Well." Goliath cleared his throat, then decided on, "If you're sure something is the right fit, why wait?" Rubbing at his chest, he admitted, "My arms feel empty when I'm not holding him. I stayed at his place Saturday night but my place last night. I kept reaching for him."

Considering Goliath had never slept a full night with anyone in his life, he decided that was damn telling.

"Wow, son." Barton chuckled softly. "I'm really happy for you."

Goliath grinned broadly. "Me, too."

They spoke for a while, Goliath sharing what he could about Earl as well as how his work was going. Seeing the time, he realized he needed to wrap it up.

"I'm meeting Earl for brunch," Goliath told his father. "I'll call you in a couple of days."

"Sounds good, son," Barton replied. After a second, he added, "I really am happy for you. I'll wait a week before booking a flight, though." He chuckled as he told him, "Give you a little time to settle into your relationship before I come tell him all your embarrassing stories."

Groaning, Goliath would forever deny the whine in his voice was he said, "Daaaaad."

Barton laughed, and they said their good-byes.

"Goliath, come into my office," Anthony called as soon as Goliath walked into the sheriff's station after his wonderful brunch with Earl.

Goliath could hardly wait until both their shifts were over, as he was heading to Earl's house for the evening. The hairs on his nape stood on end just thinking about allowing his lover to claim him. He'd only bottomed a handful of times, and it had been many years ago.

"Coming, sir," Goliath responded, changing directions.

Nereo smirked at him and winked from where he was seated behind the reception desk.

Goliath arched one brow but didn't comment as he passed. It wasn't until he was halfway across the floor that he recalled that Nereo was supposed to be a vampire. Peering over his shoulder, Goliath stared at the male's back, wondering if there was some kind of tell that he should have noticed.

*Probably not.*

"You wanted to see me, Sheriff," Goliath stated as he entered Anthony's office.

Anthony nodded. "Please shut the door and have a seat."

Goliath did as he was told and settled into a chair before

the desk.

"First things first." Anthony smiled. "Congratulations. I'm really happy for you and Earl."

"Thank you." Goliath returned the man's smile even as he rubbed the back of his neck. "I'm still a little blindsided," he admitted before relaxing back in his seat. "But Earl is amazing and . . . yeah, I'm looking forward to sharing a life with him."

Never in a million years would Goliath have thought that after only knowing someone for a few days.

"Feels surreal," Goliath whispered.

Chuckling, Anthony nodded. "I imagine it does." Then he rested his forearms on the desk and folded his hands. "Onto the next topic, then." He scowled at his desk for a few seconds before returning his attention to Goliath. "Emily was already in here this morning. She tried to file a complaint against you, Deputy Nathan, and Earl."

"Tried to?" Goliath questioned.

"Yeah, tried to," Anthony responded dryly with a roll of his eyes. "Good grief. That woman is a piece of work."

Goliath heaved a deep sigh as he frowned at the desk. "Yeah. She's definitely . . . something else," he rumbled, trying to be tactful.

"You don't seem surprised about her being here," Anthony commented, relaxing back in his seat. "I guess she made quite the spectacle at the bar Saturday night."

Heaving a sigh, Goliath admitted, "Emily was very handsy, and she didn't want to take no for an answer." He scowled at his boss and told him, "She also said some not-very nice things, telling me I'll be labeled a fag, even if I'm bisexual."

"Yeah, piece of work," Anthony repeated. "Anyway." He tapped the side of his nose. "You're aware that shifters have a more advanced sense of smell, right?"

Goliath hesitated. "I may have been told that." He'd been

told a lot of things, and not all of them had stuck.

Anthony chuckled, nodding as if understanding his unspoken thought. "Well, one of the pros at having a highly developed sense of smell is that we can tell when someone is lying to us." Scoffing, he rolled his eyes as he shook his head. "And Emily stunk to high heaven of bullshit." Crossing his arms over his chest, Anthony told him, "Anyway, I went ahead and reminded her that filing a false police report would incur a penalty. She called me a few names and scuttled out of here. But I don't think that's going to be the end of it."

"No?" Goliath wondered what the woman's deal was. "Why? Why can't she just let it go?"

"Some people are just that way," Anthony grumbled with a shake of his head. "I swear. The number of people who feel entitled to whatever they want grows exponentially every year." Reaching for his coffee mug, Anthony told him, "Anyway, be careful out there. I don't need any more deputies injured by crazy vindictive women and their friends or family."

Goliath hesitated a second, trying to understand that. Then it clicked. "Oh, Deputy Ron." He hadn't met the man, yet, as he'd been run off the road and into a ravine by someone before Goliath had arrived in town a few weeks prior. "How's he doing, anyway?"

"On the mend," Anthony told him after taking a sip of his coffee. "Lark plans to do a second surgery on his leg this week to take out the pins he put in."

"Take *out*?" Goliath asked incredulously. "Why would he do that?"

Anthony's eyes widened before he grinned. "Right. He's a wolf shifter." With a grin, he told him, "Lark put pins into his leg so it would heal properly, but he needs to take them back out again so they won't impair his ability to shift."

Goliath blew out a sharp breath. "So much more to learn."

Nodding, Anthony told him, "I'm still short-staffed, so I

can't give you a whole lot of time off for your bonding, but if you get me Earl's schedule at *Caribou's*, I'll make certain they line up."

"Thank you, Sheriff," Goliath replied, surprised at his thoughtfulness.

Anthony nodded, rising to his feet. "Of course." He reached across the table, holding out his hand. "And congratulations again."

Following Anthony's example, Goliath stood. "Thank you, sir."

After shaking the man's hand, Goliath headed out of his boss's office and started his shift.

Pulling up in front of Earl's home, Goliath threw his truck into park. He stared at the house for a moment, focusing on his breathing, trying to get his nerves under control. While Goliath wanted what the wolf shifter was offering, that didn't change the fact that it was a scary step.

Goliath threaded his hand through his hair, knocking his hat askew. Moving his cowboy hat to the back seat, he grabbed his overnight bag from the passenger floorboard. He pushed out of his vehicle, closed the door, locked it, then headed toward the house.

The door opened before Goliath even reached it. Earl stood framed in the doorway, his lean frame illuminated by the light behind him. His lover wore only a pair of sweatpants slung low on his lean hips.

"Wow," Goliath mumbled, nearly missing a step. "You are . . . so damn sexy."

Earl smiled, lifting a hand and beckoning to him. "I think the same of you, my mate."

Goliath took Earl's hand, allowing his lover to lead him inside. The other man shut the door behind them. Then he took Goliath's bag from his shoulder and drew him into the living room.

"I can scent your nerves, Goliath," Earl murmured, placing the bag on the recliner. Looking up at him, he rested his now free hand on Goliath's chest. "If you need more time, we don't have to do this tonight."

As much as Goliath appreciated the out, he didn't want it. He rested his hand on Earl's waist, using his thumb to tease along the edge of his abdominals. He felt the skin flutter underneath his hold, and he spotted the tell-tale bulge tenting Earl's sweats.

"I don't want to wait, Earl," Goliath assured him. Giving him a small smile, he admitted, "It's just been a long time since I've been on the receiving end." He scoffed softly as he glanced down at himself before returning his attention to Earl's gorgeous masculine features. "Not too many have been ballsy enough to ask."

Earl's eyes narrowed a smidge as he slipped his hand under Goliath's shirt and began tracing over his six-pack. "I'm a switch, so I can't wait to feel your gorgeous cannon in my ass, but right now . . . I need to claim you."

Goliath's lips twitched upon hearing Earl's words. "My cannon, huh?"

Winking, Earl nodded. "Oh, yeah." He squeezed Goliath's hand before releasing him, moving his palm to cup Goliath through his jeans. "Definitely a cannon."

Grunting, Goliath bucked his hips, pushing into Earl's hold. "Damn," he muttered. "You work me up so fucking fast."

"Then let me help you take the edge off, my mate," Earl purred even as he lowered to his knees. He reached for the fly of Goliath's jeans before pausing to peer at him through his lashes. "You okay with doing it out here? In front of the fire?"

Goliath barely spared the dancing flames in the hearth a glance. He was too entranced by the lovely view of Earl on his knees before him, offering to pleasure him. It was a sight Goliath knew he would never tire of.

"Y-Yeah." Goliath sucked in a harsh breath as he clenched his abs, offering Earl's agile fingers more room to work. "This is perfect."

"You're perfect," Earl countered, making quick work of Goliath's fly. "Absolutely perfect."

"Don't know about that," Goliath muttered as he watched Earl lower his jeans to mid-thigh, followed by his underwear. The feel of his erection freed from his boxer-briefs drew a relieved groan from between his lips. Seeing Earl lick his lips, Goliath pleaded, "Please suck me."

Earl grinned up at him, his dark eyes seeming to glow with some inner light. "With pleasure."

Then Earl opened his mouth, wrapped his lips around Goliath's broad mushroom head, and suckled. The sweet suction caused tingles to erupt over the flesh of his groin, and his skin goose bumped. A full-body shiver went through him, and he couldn't resist threading his fingers through Earl's thick blond hair.

"Earl," Goliath whispered roughly.

Peering at him through his lashes, Earl smiled obscenely around his cock head. He held Goliath's gaze as he slowly sank onto his erection, swallowing him to the root. When Earl's nose was buried in Goliath's bush, he sucked and hummed, sending vibrations cascading along his sensitive length.

Goliath groaned upon feeling the delicious stimulation. The muscles of his abdominals fluttered beyond his control. His body, too keyed up from anticipation, went up in flames.

When Earl cradled his balls while lodging his knob in the back of his throat, swallowing around it, it was game over.

Shouting Earl's name, Goliath tightened his hold as his body bowed. His thighs shook as his balls pulled tight. He lost any semblance of control, his hips rocking. Fucking Earl's mouth once, twice, then he came, pouring his seed into his lover's hot, sucking mouth.

"Earl!"

# CHAPTER TWELVE

Earl swallowed every shot of Goliath's delicious cream. His wolf howled with satisfaction that they'd made their human come from so little stimulation. Silently agreeing with his animal, Earl gave his mate's jerking penis a couple more suckles, making certain he'd milked him for every last drop.

Finally, Earl slid his fingers along Goliath's fingers where they were tangled in his hair. He helped his mate ease his grip before he gently pulled off his lover's prick. Seeing Goliath's knees tremble, a fresh wash of pride flooded him.

Returning his hold to Goliath's hips, Earl helped steady his lover. "Come lie on this blanket with me," he encouraged, glancing toward the blanket he'd spread before the fire before his mate had arrived. "I'll undress you, and help you relax while I open you up."

Goliath nodded even as he fingered Earl's hair, threading his fingers through his locks. "Love running my fingers through your hair," he murmured, peering at him with a sated, heavy-lidded gaze. "So pretty."

Earl hummed, smiling appreciatively. "So glad to hear that. Love your touch." He rose to his feet and gripped the hem of Goliath's shirt. "Let's take this off."

With a quick nod, Goliath took the hem from Earl's hands. He whipped it over his head and tossed it aside. Goliath followed that up by gripping his jeans and shuffling to the blanket Earl had indicated. Settling with his bare ass on the soft comforter, he bent his knees and reached for the laces of his boots.

Settling near Goliath's feet, Earl untied his mate's second boot. He pulled it off and set it aside, his human doing the same with his other one. Once his socks were tugged off, Earl followed that up by removing Goliath's jeans and underwear.

Once nude, Goliath rested his forearms on his upturned knees and peered at him questioningly.

Earl noticed the slight hint of nerves once again began to tease his nostrils. Not liking that, he leaned over and grabbed a tub of massage oil he'd left near the hearth right next to the lube. Next, Earl picked up a hand towel and held it out.

"Roll over and relax on your stomach," Earl encouraged. "Put this under your groin." Showing off the oil, he told him, "I'm going to give you a massage for a few minutes before I start slicking you up."

Goliath chuckled softly even as he took the towel and obeyed. "Sounds like you're gonna slick me up in a couple of ways."

Then Goliath winked and sprawled on the blanket. After tucking the towel under his groin, letting out a soft hiss in the process, he folded his arms and rested his cheek upon them. Goliath tipped his head to the side just enough to watch him out of one eye.

Earl had taken advantage of Goliath's movements to kick off his own sweatpants. Kneeling nude beside his mate, he unscrewed the jar. He dipped his fingers into the tub and scooped out a generous portion, which he rubbed between his palms, slicking up his hands.

Returning his attention to Goliath, Earl nearly swallowed his tongue. His mate lay before him, tall, broad, and heavily muscled. He admired the man's thick lines and smooth flesh. Earl had enjoyed the opportunity to explore Goliath over the weekend, and he couldn't wait to do it all over again.

So he didn't.

Settling his hands on Goliath's shoulders, Earl began working his human's muscles. He rubbed and kneaded, pushed and pulled. Finding knots here and there, Earl took his time to ease each one, working down his spine and across the wide expanse of his torso. He reveled in each hum and groan drawn from his lover, and it wasn't long until his mate was a puddle of goo beneath his fingers.

Earl reached Goliath's lower back and used a knee to encourage his mate to spread his legs. His human obeyed, allowing him to move between his thighs. He added more oil to his hands before starting on Goliath's hips, moving down the hard muscles of his ass.

Finally, Earl began teasing his thumbs along Goliath's trench while working the base of his globes. He began rubbing lightly at his mate's entrance as he kneaded the tops of his thighs. Alternating his hands, Earl dipped his thumb deeper and deeper into Goliath's hole.

To Earl's relief, it didn't take long before Goliath mumbled, "More, Earl. I need more."

Earl gave it to him. Moving his left hand up to the small of Goliath's back, he rubbed soothingly. He sank the forefinger of his right hand into Goliath's chute, deeper and deeper. Feeling no resistance, just blessedly tight heat, Earl uttered a moan of his own as his aching erection twitched in anticipation.

"Oh, gods," Earl groaned, wanting inside Goliath in the worst way. As he began finger-fucking his mate with first one finger, then two, he murmured, "You're going to squeeze me so perfect, my mate. Can hardly wait."

"Hurry," Goliath growled. "Need you, damn it."

Suddenly, Earl registered something he should have noticed before, but it had built up slowly. The room was flooded with the delicious aroma of Goliath's renewed arousal. Earl inhaled deeply, taking in the ball-tingling fragrance.

"Oh fuck," Earl whined, quickly moving his left hand to the base of his dick. He squeezed tightly, reverently whispering his mate's name. "Goliath. My mate." Earl quickly slid a third digit inside Goliath beside the first two. "Have you been playing with yourself?" he couldn't help but ask.

Earl noticed the faintest scent of embarrassment even as Goliath admitted, "Yeah. While in the shower."

Groaning, Earl imagined that and nearly came. He had to squeeze the base of his dick to the point of pain to ease his need. Once he had himself under control, he eased his fingers free of Goliath's chute.

Goliath groaned and turned his head farther, watching him.

Leaning over, Earl grabbed the lube. He quickly spurted some directly onto his dick. After swiping along his length twice, he gripped his base as he levered over his mate.

When Goliath made a move as if to rise to his knees, Earl rested a palm in the middle of his back. "Stay still," he urged, rubbing gently. "Wanna sprawl on your big, sexy body."

Relaxing once more, Goliath nodded in agreement.

Earl took that as the permission it was. Adjusting his position, he placed a knee outside each of Goliath's thighs, encouraging him to close his legs just a smidge. Then he rested his hand on the comforter under his mate's armpit while pointing his cock toward his lover's hole.

Lowering closer, Earl touched his crown to Goliath's opening. He felt goose bumps break out on his thighs. Gritting his teeth, he pushed his hips forward, applying pressure.

With Goliath uttering a soft grunt, his body gave way.

Gasping at the exquisite pressure of Goliath's hot body swallowing his crown, Earl whispered his mate's name. Unable to stop, he sank deeper and deeper. His gut clenched as he bottomed out, his balls resting against the crease where his lover's ass met his thighs.

"Oh, fuck," Earl murmured, a shiver rolling through him. He sprawled over Goliath, allowing the much larger man to take his weight. Pressed together from thigh to shoulders, Earl nuzzled his cheek against Goliath's upper back. "So good."

"Earl," Goliath muttered. He reached down and back, grabbing Earl's hand. Pulling his hand up near his head, he threaded their fingers together. Squeezing, he ordered, "Move, baby. Please move."

Groaning, Earl obeyed. "Anything for you, my mate."

Crunching his abs, Earl began to move. He withdrew his erection slowly until his flared crown nudged the tight ring of his mate's outer ring. Then he snapped his hips forward, burying his prick as deeply as possible.

Earl moaned roughly, the sensations cascading over the length of his dick going straight to his balls. His groin tingled, and his body flushed hot. Unable to help himself, Earl gave in to his need and began a harsh fucking, stabbing into his mate over and over again.

Pain and pleasure swirled together, the heat and squeeze almost too much as he hammered into Goliath again and again. Shudders racked him, and he tangled the fingers of his free hand into the comforter beneath them. Only his instinct to never hurt his mate allowed Earl to keep the fingers twined with his mate's reasonably relaxed.

"Oh, fuck!" Goliath cried, his big body jolting beneath him.

Memorizing that spot, Earl began to repeatedly peg his lover's gland. The growls, grunts, and groans were music to his ears. The smell of masculine sweat, arousal, and need flooded his nostrils.

When Earl scented the tangy fragrance of Goliath's cum, his balls pulled impossibly tighter. His release bowled through his system, and his seed gushed from him. Earl's release rushed from him in hard bliss-inducing spurts, making his senses sing and black spots to dance before his eyes.

With his head spinning, Earl couldn't have stayed his instinct to claim even if he'd wanted to — which he didn't. His canines lengthened, and his mouth watered. Easing his still-twitching prick free of Goliath's body, he scooted up his big mate's body. Earl tucked his face in the crook of his mate's neck and struck, sinking his teeth deep into his mate.

Goliath jerked underneath him as his rich, tasty nectar flowed up around his teeth. Earl licked around his embedded teeth before sucking hard. Groaning against Goliath's sweaty flesh, he reveled in his mate's iron-rich flavor.

After one more suck, Earl felt Goliath shudder beneath him. His mate groaned his name, squeezing their twined fingers tightly. The tangy fragrance of more of his seed flooded the air.

Earl moaned around the flesh he sucked, the mixture quickly going to his head ... and his balls. To his shock, his cock throbbed and his balls tingled. After one more gulp of Goliath's life-giving ambrosia, a second orgasm blind-sided Earl, sending his senses reeling.

As Earl floated on waves of ecstasy, he had just enough presence of mind to ease his teeth free of Goliath's neck. Humming happily, he licked over his mate's flesh, sealing the wound. As he drifted, he admired the beautiful claiming scar he'd left behind.

Finally, Earl began to gather some semblance of coherence. He turned his head and nuzzled his cheek against the column of Goliath's neck. His mate's smooth warm skin and masculine fragrance infused him. Feeling their completed bond, Earl couldn't ever remember feeling more content.

"Holy shit," Goliath mumbled. He turned and lifted his head, eyeing him awkwardly. "That was fucking amazing."

Earl chuckled before winking at Goliath. "I think you mean it was some amazing fucking."

Barking a laugh, Goliath grinned at him as he squeezed their twined fingers. "You made my cannon fire more times than I ever thought possible." As he spoke, he waggled his eyebrows.

Dissolving into laughter, Earl clutched his mate. He couldn't ever remember a time when he'd felt so giddy and so relaxed at the same time. Earl hadn't ever had such fun with sex before.

The trill of Earl's phone pulled him out of his mirth. Recognizing his alpha's ringtone, he frowned. With a groan, he eased off Goliath's back, hissing a little when their quickly drying semen — thanks to the nearby fire — tugged at his pubic hairs.

"Seriously?" Goliath grumbled, releasing his hand.

"Sorry," Earl murmured apologetically, gaining his hands and knees. Offering a commiserating smile, he explained, "That's Declan's ringtone. I need to get this."

Goliath winced even as he nodded.

Earl started crawling toward his phone, which he'd left on the coffee table.

"You don't need to get that."

Snapping his attention toward the feminine voice, Earl froze. He spotted Emily standing in his foyer. While she was in the process of closing the front door, she also held a beat-up .22 rifle on them.

"It's so funny how often us hicks leave our doors unlocked, isn't it?" Emily stated as if they were having an everyday conversation. "Us country folk are far too trusting." When she grinned, the expression appeared a little deranged. "You really should have let me have Goliath when you had the chance, Earl. Now . . . I'm going to kill you." Shaking her head, Emily curled her lip as she swept her gaze over them. "I *was* going to let you live, Goliath. I wanted you for myself, after all." She held up a syringe containing a sickly green liquid, showing it to them, before placing it on the side table near the door. "I can't pronounce it, but it's a lovely chemical that puts the person into a suggestive state. I would have *suggested* that you were just being polite but never really wanted Earl. You really want me." Emily's expression once again morphed into distaste. "But, now that I know you let Earl fuck you, Goliath, you need to die, too."

"You really don't want to do this, Emily," Earl murmured. He mentally judged the distance between them, wondering if he could cross it swiftly enough to take her out before she managed to shoot Goliath. "You'll never get away with it."

*As long as I stay between her and Goliath, I can do this.*

Earl tensed, preparing to leap to his feet and sprint across the room.

Emily's eyes narrowed, and she lifted the rifle to her shoulder. "Ah, ah, ah," she tsked. "I know it doesn't look like much. Just a small game rifle really, but it shoots true." Smiling coldly, Emily added, "And just like most hicks around here, I've been hunting since I was eight, and I'm a great shot."

Seeing that the .22 was pointed at Goliath, Earl froze.

*Shit!*

"Isn't it funny." A deep voice filled the air right before Nereo appeared with vampire speed. The male grabbed the barrel of the rifle and pushed it toward the ceiling. At the same time, he wrapped his arm around Emily from behind, clutching her back to his chest before wrenching the gun from her grip. As Nereo grinned at Earl, showing off his fangs, he finished his thought. "How often us hicks leave our doors unlocked, isn't it?"

Emily shrieked, bucking in Nereo's hold. "Let go of me," she demanded.

She attempted to stomp on his foot and kick him in the balls, but the vampire was far too fast for her.

"Now, now, Emily," Nereo chided. "You're under arrest

for attempted murder." He tossed the rifle on the sofa and picked up the syringe. "And because we don't want you to remember my speed" — he used his teeth to yank the cap off the needle before stabbing it into the neck of the screaming, wriggling woman — "there we go. Poetic justice."

After an instant, Emily grew lax in Nereo's grip, her eyes glazing.

"How did you move like that?" Goliath asked, clearly shocked.

Nereo grinned again. "Vampire trait, Goliath. We're super speedy." He winked as he swept his gaze over them before smirking at Earl. "And you might want to call Declan back. Otherwise, he's going to head over here to check on you." Tossing Emily over his shoulder, Nereo added, "Just let him know I neutralized the problem."

"Wait, how did you know?" Earl waved toward Emily. "About her?"

With a roll of his eyes, Nereo told them, "Anthony wanted to keep an eye on her, so I was surveilling her. I saw her pull out her .22 and overheard enough of her rantings to figure out her plan." He frowned as he shook his head. "Don't worry. We'll come up with something plausible and let you know what your statements need to be."

Then, with a wave, Nereo let himself out the still-open front door and disappeared into the night, closing the door behind him.

"Huh."

Earl jumped to his feet and quickly locked the door. Then he turned back to face Goliath. His mate had flipped the comforter over his groin, and he stared up at Earl in bewilderment.

"You okay?" Earl asked, crossing back to his mate and kneeling before him. He took his lover's hand, needing the connection of touch to comfort not just himself but his wolf.

Unable to help himself, Earl admitted, "Seeing that rifle aimed at you scared the ever-loving shit out of me."

Goliath chuckled softly as he squeezed their hands. "I'm fine, Earl," he assured. With a wry smile, he told him, "I was sitting here trying to figure out a way to push you out of the way while still being able to get to her."

Grinning, Earl felt touched even as he was beyond grateful for Nereo's intervention.

"I'm glad neither of us had to deal with it," Earl murmured, leaning close and touching his lips to Goliath's.

Earl had intended to deepen the kiss, to tumble his mate back to the floor and perhaps start another round. Unfortunately, the trill of the phone interrupted him once again. With a groan, Earl drew away and reached for it.

Goliath chuckled roughly as he shoved the comforter aside. "Answer the phone," he encouraged as he climbed to his feet. "I'm going to go get something to clean us up with. Then we'll curl up and talk about how difficult it'll be to move me in here."

His breath catching in his throat, a feeling of rightness flooded Earl. As he watched his naked mate stroll from the room, he picked up the phone. Absently, Earl answered, content in the knowledge that his mate would soon be back, and he would be able to hold him every day and night for the rest of his days.

*Nothing could be more perfect.*

# ABOUT THE AUTHOR

Charlie started writing fantasy when she was eight, and after stumbling onto her first erotic romance at age nineteen, she realized her true calling. She now focuses on writing gay erotic romance, normally of the paranormal variety, with heroes of all kinds. With the help and support of her husband, Charlie finally fulfilled one of her life-long goals . . . move to acreage with her horses. You can often find her curled up with her laptop and a cup of tea or glass of wine, creating her next adventure. Charlie enjoys exploring the mountains of her new Oregon home on horseback, 4-wheeler, or motorcycle.

She can be reached at ch.richards2010@yahoo.com

Or visit her at www.charlie-richards.com.